Tell the Truth, Cassie

Renée Kent

ADVENTURES IN MISTY FALLS

6

Tell the Truth, Cassie

Renée Kent

New Hope® Publishers

Birmingham, Alabama

New Hope® Publishers
P.O. Box 12065
Birmingham, AL 35202-2065
www.newhopepubl.com

Library of Congress Cataloging-in-Publication Data

Kent, Renée Holmes, 1955-
  Tell the truth, Cassie / Renée Kent.
       p. cm. -- (Adventures in Misty Falls ; bk. 6)
Summary: Cassie wants so much to be on the school track team that she
copies from J.J. on a test and lies to her teachers and parents, but a
poster of the Ten Commandments and a disaster remind her to do what is
right.
  ISBN 1-56309-452-5 (pbk.)
  [1. Track and field--Fiction. 2. Cheating--Fiction. 3.Honesty--Fiction.
4. Christian life--Fiction. 5. Schools--Fiction.] I. Title.
  PZ7.K419 Te 2000
  [Fic]--dc21
                                              00-011211

Cover design by Todd Cotton
Cover illustration by Matt Archambault

ISBN: 1-56309-452-5
N007106 • 1000 • 7.5M1

Misty Falls, Georgia

Tell the Truth, Cassie

1

"Cock-a-doodle-doo!"

What a loud way to wake up on a crisp, autumn morning! The most annoying gift Cassie Holbrook had ever received began to crow noisily right in her upstairs bedroom.

No, a real rooster was not perched on Cassie's bookshelf. The week before, her family had given her a very rude, plastic rooster alarm clock. Cassie groaned. Her dreams had been full of romping, baby horses. Running through the Misty Falls meadows with horses was much more fun than crawling out of a comfy, warm bed.

"Cock-a-doodle-doo! Cock-a-doodle-doo! Cock-a-doodle-doo! Cock-a-doodle-doo!" Each crow seemed louder than the one before it.

Then a chorus began. Opie, Cassie's black and white Jack Russell terrier, scrambled into the room, barking furiously at the rooster. Next, he ran to Cassie's bedside and barked at her, as if to ask, Don't you hear that? What are you going to do about it?

Back and forth across the room, Opie ran. His tail wagged so excitedly that his whole body wiggled from side to side. The rooster crowed while Opie barked.

Even with an out-of-tune animal chorus blaring in her ears, Cassie's body still refused to uncurl itself and greet the new day.

In her swirl of rumpled covers, she grumbled again at the irritating sound. Her light auburn hair scattered in long, disorderly strands, as she buried her face deeper into her nest of soft pillows.

Let me sleep! Cassie begged, in her thoughts. Then she said aloud, "Opie, ssshh!" Louder she added, "Somebody please turn off the rooster!"

But no one came to rescue her. The rooster alarm insisted that she "rise and shine," as Mother always put it. She sighed hopelessly. This was sheer torture...by far and away the most annoying way for a growing eleven-year-old to wake up on a Saturday morning—or any other morning, for that matter. In Cassie's opinion, the crack of dawn was no time to "rise and shine."

But even Cassie had to admit that the rooster, with Opie's help, was the only alarm clock that truly did its job—waking up its new owner. Cassie didn't see it as a good thing at all. Why her family had given her the silly rooster clock in the first place was a mystery to her.

Tell the Truth, Cassie

After all, just because she had trouble waking up in time for school didn't seem like a very good reason to irritate her with a cock-a-doodling rooster every morning. Over and over and over, it insisted that Cassie get up. By now, Opie had grown even more excited, echoing every single "cock-a-doodle-doo" with a quicker series of ear-piercing barks. Even though she tried to convince her body to get out of bed and turn off the alarm, her legs refused to budge.

Finally, she whimpered and rolled over with a frown on her sleepy, freckled face. She opened one hazel eye and squinted at Opie, then at the crowing plastic clock. From its perch on the shelf above her cluttered study desk, its red beak and orange and yellow tail feathers moved about mechanically as it crowed. The face of the clock read "6:38." The rooster had been crowing eight whole minutes. It had seemed like much longer than that.

Cassie tried to move again, but her body still felt like a wet noodle, but she then noticed movement in the hall. She was glad to see her brother Jeff peering into the doorway. He was rubbing his freshly washed, dark hair with a hand towel. When he had finished, he looked like a porcupine, with short spikes pro-truding all over his head.

"Oh good, Jeff, please turn off my alarm for me. I'm awake!" Cassie tried hard to make her voice carry a sweet tone. To her dismay, the rooster continued its squawky serenade. Worse, Jeff made no move to turn off the alarm. He quieted Opie, though, by scratching him behind the ears.

Cassie tried to remember why Jeff would be up and dressed already this morning. That's right, she remembered, he has football practice. Ever since he was the only freshman who had made the starting varsity lineup, Jeff had no trouble bounding out of bed each day.

Finally, her brother spoke with irritation, but his voice had that teasing tone. "Get a clue, Sis. That bird is not going to stop crowing, until YOU turn it off."

Then he threw the towel like a football at Cassie. It landed with a wet smack in the middle of her face.

"Ow!" she sputtered, as tiny water droplets sprayed on her mouth, freckled nose, and cheeks. "What's the big idea? Jeff, be nice for a change. Please turn off the alarm for me."

"Cock-a-doodle-doo!" crowed the rooster. As she suspected, he wasn't about to turn off her alarm. Now it was payback time—her turn to throw the towel at her older brother. As she drew back her arm to take aim, she hoped it would hit him in the nose, but he easily caught the towel in midair.

Jeff sniffed with an amused twinkle in his eye. "It's your alarm clock, not mine," he said. "Gotta go. We're watching the tape from last night's big win! Misty Falls Mustangs rule! See ya. C'mon, Opie."

With that, he scooped up all eighteen pounds of Opie, who had grown weary of the pesky rooster, and they disappeared down the stairs.

"Cock-a-doodle-doo! Cock-a-doodle-doo!"

Cassie huffed, puffed, and groaned a huge "Ohhhhh!" Finally, she rolled out of bed before that rooster could crow one more time. She rubbed the sand out of her eyes and stumbled blindly toward the bookshelf.

On the way, she tried to untwist her pajama bottoms, which were wrapped twice around her waist. *Wow*, she thought. She had noticed lately that all her clothes had been hanging loosely. Running two miles each night after chores with her best friend, J.J., had really slimmed her up!

On tiptoes, Cassie reached for the "off" button on the rooster's back. "Cock-a-doodle-doo" said the rooster, as it shut down before finishing its final call.

Whew! Sweet silence at last! She breathed a sigh of relief just as her mother stepped into the room.

"Well, it's about time!" her mom exclaimed, taking a sip of her morning coffee. "I could hear that thing hollering all the way downstairs in the kitchen. But never mind that. Mission accomplished. I'm pleased to see that your new alarm clock has finally gotten you up and going."

"Uh-huh," yawned Cassie, trying not to feel cranky. She walked heavily back toward the bed.

But Mom stopped her. "Now don't you even think about going back to bed, Cassie Marie Holbrook, or you'll miss track team tryouts."

Suddenly, every muscle and bone in her body was 100 percent wide awake. Now she remembered why her alarm was set so early on a Saturday!

This was the big day she and J.J. had been waiting for. A little later this morning, they would try out for the Misty Falls Middle School track team. She really hoped she would make the cut. She wasn't quite as strong as J.J. for long runs, or as fast as Iggy Potts or Hunter Harris. For a sprinter, though, she wasn't half bad.

"I hope Coach Blevins notices how hard I've been working on my sprints," Cassie said. She waited for her mom to express how proud she was of her youngest daughter's efforts to improve her speed.

But Mom was frowning, as she looked around the messy room. Cassie noticed instantly. Suddenly she began to see her room through her mom's eyes and felt shame wash over her.

A sharp, testy note was in Mom's voice. "Cassie Marie, I ever so carefully ironed and folded your clean clothes. Why are they now scattered all over the floor and mixed with the dirty ones? And why is a granola bar wrapper wadded up on your nightstand? And this empty glass with dried milk in the bottom too?"

"Well, uh," Cassie said, feeling sheepish, as she

silently hoped her mom hadn't seen the shriveled banana peel on the dresser. She couldn't think of a good excuse. Food upstairs was off limits at the Holbrook house. And there was no denying that she was supposed to have placed her fresh laundry in the drawers—not sprinkled all over the floor.

Mom's hands were on her hips now. "Dirty clothes belong in the hamper. Clean clothes belong in the drawers. Food is to be eaten in the kitchen only. Get a move on, young lady."

"Yes, ma'am," said Cassie meekly. She knew when she had been caught red-handed.

"You'll be allowed to go to track tryouts only after you clean up your room and do your chores in the barn. Remember the ground rules that you agreed to abide by when your father and I gave our permission for you to try out for track."

Now it was Cassie's turn to frown. "How could I forget?" Then she counted on her fingers as she stated aloud the ground rules Mom was referring to. "Keep my room clean at all times. Faithfully do my other chores, including washing the dog once a week and scrubbing the tub each time I use it."

"And?" Mom asked, waiting patiently. "What about studies?"

"Oh yes," said Cassie with a sigh. "Keep up with school assignments and turn in all homework on time."

"That's my girl," said Mom. Her cloud of disapproval had vanished as quickly as it had come. She headed out of the room, saying, "Now, come down for breakfast as soon as you can. I'm keeping it warm for you, but I don't want your eggs to get stiff."

"Thank you," said Cassie. She gazed at the mess in her room. How would she ever get this cleaned up in time for track—and take care of her pony too?

Secretly, she wished that life didn't have to have so many rules and regulations. She was tired of always obeying. She just wanted to have fun—and be a track star!

Cassie dressed in record time. The night before, she had laid out what she would wear to tryouts—a pair of red shorts, a white tank, and a long-sleeved T-shirt with "I LOVE TRACK" printed across it. She put her hair in a ponytail and finished off the look with a yellow sweatband across her forehead, her sports socks, and brand-new running shoes that Dad had bought for her last Saturday.

Next, she tackled her room. The clean clothes that were sprawled all over the floor were covered with Opie's hair. She refolded most of the clean clothes, dusting off dog hair as she went. She stuffed them into her bureau drawers, then tossed all her shoes into a pile in the closet and closed the door.

A few CDs and girls' sports magazines that she and J.J. had been looking at lay on the floor next to her bed. With one foot, she scooted them under the dust ruffle, so that they wouldn't show.

Then she stared at her study desk, piled high with an assortment of—well, stuff. She couldn't decide how to make order of it. It looked as though a windstorm had scattered all sorts of things across her room and onto the desk. She opened the top drawer of the desk.

It might all fit in there, she said to herself.

With her arm, she raked everything together into the drawer. Into the drawer went a sock, pencils, markers, snapshots of her friends, pens, a couple of dead batteries from her flashlight, some old homework papers, hair bands, a pair of gym shorts, her house key, several coins, her pre-algebra book, a watch, and two bottles of J.J.'s nail polish.

The top of the desk was now clear, neat, and orderly, except for some dust. Cassie took the gym shorts back out of the drawer and wiped away the dust. Now the surface was shiny too!

Ah-choo! Cassie sneezed.

Next she threw the dusty gym shorts into the drawer with everything else and tried to close it. As a matter of fact, she tried three times, but the drawer was just too full to close properly.

Cassie didn't give up, though. She opened the second drawer and transferred some of the things into it. There. Both drawers would close properly now. She would just have to clean out those drawers when she had more time. Mother would never have to know.

Standing back to admire her work, she realized all of a sudden that she had forgotten to make her bed. So she pulled up the bedspread over the rumpled sheets and blanket and fluffed her pillows. She placed an array of stuffed animals on top of the rumply spots in the bed. The bed now looked like a small zoo.

The only thing left to do was trash duty. She collected the granola bar wrapper, the black banana peel, a gum wrapper, and some movie ticket stubs and tossed them in her trashcan. She picked up the dirty milk glass to take to the kitchen sink and stood in the doorway to inspect her job.

Her room cleaning wasn't perfect by any means, but it would satisfy Mom for today. That is, if her mom didn't check her work too closely. As she scampered downstairs, Cassie promised herself that she would do a much better job next time.

Being excited about tryouts and eating breakfast just didn't seem to go together. Cassie managed to take two bites of warm eggs and satisfied her mother's worries about "good nutrition" by guzzling a cup of orange juice to wash down her vitamin pill. She had only five minutes left to turn the horses out to graze and clean the stalls. *I'll never make it*, she thought.

To save time, Cassie decided to clean the stalls that

Tell the Truth, Cassie

afternoon, after she returned from track tryouts. Besides, she didn't want to get her new shoes and her track clothes dirty. So she turned out her spotted, poky pony, Chester, and J.J.'s sleek mare, Gracie, into the pasture to graze on the thick green grass that seemed to thrive in the dewy fall morning air. The horses can drink fresh water from Possum Creek, she reasoned. And by tonight, she could supply them with fresh bedding, grain, hay, and water in their stalls.

Cassie led Gracie by her lead rope to the pasture. Chester followed obediently. Holding Gracie's halter, Cassie unlatched the lead rope and laid it over the fence railing.

As soon as the gate opened, Chester and Gracie ran and kicked gleefully into the field, just as they had every morning. Meanwhile, J.J. and her mother drove up the driveway and beeped the horn at Cassie. She waved at them. Then she closed the pasture gate firmly and locked it. She sprinted to the car and climbed inside.

As the car pulled out of the driveway, the girls and Ms. Graystone laughed at the horses' antics. Chester and Gracie were the best of equine friends, nipping playfully at each other's necks and running headlong toward their favorite grazing spot.

As the car entered the middle school parking lot, J.J. and Cassie looked at each other for a long

11

moment and then squealed in unison. That was code for "This is it! The time has come! Are you as excited as I am?"

As Cassie unfastened her seatbelt, she pointed at the printed message on her shirt. "I love track!" she exclaimed, half-reading.

J.J. giggled. Her cheeks were rosy with anticipation. "If we both make the team, we'll have so much fun together," she said.

Cassie opened the car door, nodded, and said, "Don't we always have fun? Thanks for giving me a ride, Ms. Graystone!"

"My pleasure," said J.J.'s mom. "I hope you'll both be selected for the track team."

"Oh, I'm sure J.J. will," said Cassie, patting her friend on the arm. "She has the highest endurance of any girl in school, even the eighth-graders."

"I'm sure Cassie will," said J.J., her violet eyes sparkling. "One day she'll be an Olympic sprinter."

"Yeah, right," giggled Cassie. She knew that J.J. was just trying to build her confidence. And maybe, just maybe...it was working!

Tell the Truth, Cassie

2

The two friends ran behind the school toward the outdoor track and field. As they jogged down the long rolling hill, they could see that Coach Blevins was already circling everybody up for roll call.

Cassie was glad that their last names fell sort of toward the middle of the alphabet. He was already calling the "B" names by the time they made it to the circle and sat down with the other girls and guys.

"Booker…Nathan Boyd…Briggs, " said Coach Blevins, checking his roster. Cassie looked around as the coach went through the roll call. What a large group they all made! There must have been about forty or fifty of them!

"All right, where's Evans?" asked Coach Blevins, looking up from his clipboard.

"Here," said Luke Evans, raising his hand.

"Oh yeah. All right, Jessica Ewing…Missy Foster…Manuel Gonzalez…Tim Freedman… Graystone….

"Here," said J.J.

"Hampton...Harris...."

"Here," said Hunter Harris. As his eager brown hand shot up, he nodded at the girls, who had just sat down directly across the circle from him. Iggy Potts, by his buddy's side, made a funny freckled face at them. J.J. and Cassie tried not to make any noise, as they held back giggles.

"Holbrook," called Coach Blevins.

"Oh! Right here, Coach," said Cassie, a little startled. Iggy's funny face had made her nearly forget to listen for her name!

Finally, "Quincy," the last name on the roster, was called. By that time, everyone had started to squirm. Cassie was starting to feel that she might burst with anticipation, if they didn't hurry up and get on with tryouts. But Coach Blevins didn't seem to be in a big rush at all.

He set down his clipboard and cleared his throat. He seemed pleased that everyone was present and accounted for. Speaking in a serious tone, the coach addressed them. "All right. Today's the day we've all been waiting for, and it's your big chance to show me what you can do out there. I'm real proud of the way each of you has worked every day after school."

Then, Coach Blevins looked in Cassie's and J.J.'s direction. He said, "Over the past few weeks, I've seen all of you improve your speed, strength, and endurance."

Tell the Truth, Cassie

Cassie felt her heart skip a beat. J.J. nudged Cassie and grinned. That meant, "See? I told you that you were getting faster!" Cassie had to smile. Her friend J.J. was such a great, encouraging friend to have around.

The girls continued to listen to their coach. "Today, I'll be choosing the best of the best for this school year's boys' and girls' track teams. Now be prepared that some of you will be named alternates. Alternates will not be required to attend all practices and meets but will be encouraged to continue training. You may be needed at any time as a replacement."

A murmur floated through the crowd of boys and girls. Everybody knew what "alternates" meant— those who didn't make the team…benchwarmers…

rejects. Cassie felt her throat tighten as she thought of not making the team. Being a "bench-warmer" was not what she had in mind at all.

She wanted to be named officially to the track team, just like she knew Hunter, Iggy, and J.J. would be. She wasn't as sure about her own abilities. There was no guarantee that she would make it. After all, she certainly wasn't one of the fastest or strongest in the group—she was just sort of "medium."

"Now," continued the coach, holding up his hand to quiet everyone, "for those of you who are named to the alternate list, I don't want this to discourage you from keeping up your training. You've all earned my respect as athletes, and you are all fine young people."

"Then why cut anyone from the team?" The question came from Hunter Harris. Cassie smiled. Even though Hunter was only in the sixth grade, his track and field skills were already among the best in the whole middle school. Besides that, he was a natural-born leader.

Ever since she had met Hunter at New Hope Center (where his little sister, Madison, received therapy for her deafness), Cassie had noticed he always looked out for others. There was no doubt in anyone's mind that Hunter was going to be selected for the boys' team. Cassie knew that he wasn't worried about himself. He was thinking of everyone else, including her.

"Good question, Harris," said Coach Blevins. He always called them by their last names. "The truth is there just aren't enough spots on the girls' and boys' track teams for everyone who has shown an interest. We're going to have to assign some of you to the alternates list. But that could change at any time! It is possible for an alternate to be named later to the team roster."

A hush fell over the crowd of track team hopefuls. Coach Blevins explained, "What that means is this: an alternate could be called in to replace a team member. Team members will be expected to abide by three rules, or risk losing their spots on the team to alternates."

Tell the Truth, Cassie

Oh no. More rules to follow, Cassie couldn't help thinking. But whatever they were, they would be worth doing to be on the track team.

"Rule Number One: Track team members will be required to attend all practices and meets," said Coach Blevins. "Rule Number Two: Track team members will conduct themselves as good citizens. And finally, Rule Number Three: Track team members will be expected to perform well in their studies."

Iggy Potts' hand shot up. "How well?" he asked. The morning sunlight seemed to radiate off his red hair.

Coach Blevins smiled at Iggy's question, and then his expression became serious again. "All track team members will be expected to score an average of C or higher on all academic work. If your grade averages in your academic subjects slip below a C for any reason, an alternate will be called in to replace you on the team."

Cassie's mind raced with this new information. Following these rules would be easy—a piece of cake. She knew she would have no problem attending track practices and meets, and she was a very good citizen. She never did anything to harm anyone or anything else, at least not intentionally.

For a moment, she considered her grades. On her first report card of the school year, she had made all Bs and one C+.

The C+ was in pre-algebra. Not too bad, but she

was going to improve that. Since J.J. always made straight As in pre-algebra, she and Cassie could do their homework assignments together in the Holbrook kitchen over warm cups of cocoa.

If she discovered that she needed extra help, Cassie could always go to her pre-algebra teacher after school—none other than Coach Blevins! Aside from being a great coach, he was a really fun teacher in class.

Cassie inhaled excitedly. Everything was in order. Today, all she had to do was prove to the coach that she belonged on the girls' Misty Falls Middle School track team!

"Any more questions before we do our warm-up exercises?" asked Coach Blevins.

"I have one more question, Coach," said Iggy. "When will we know whether we have made the team?"

Coach Blevins nodded and said, "All right, listen up. A list will be posted by 5:00 this afternoon on the front door of the middle school. All track team members will report to our first official meeting Monday after school. At that time, I will give you a list of track practices and meets that you will be expected to attend. Those who are named alternates will be welcome to come, but attendance is not required."

Since there were no more questions, Coach Blevins said, "All right boys, you come with me. Girls, you'll warm up with our new assistant, Miss Jablonski. She has come from a nearby university to help us out with training and some of our meets. We're really glad to have you, Miss Jablonski."

They hadn't noticed the new assistant until then. She had been standing outside the circle, behind J.J. and Cassie. The girls twisted around to see her. Miss Jablonski's long, blonde hair was pulled back into a ponytail, and her smile was as bright as the lady's on the toothpaste commercial on TV. Cassie liked her right away.

"Hi, everybody," she said in a friendly voice. "It's great to be here. I'm looking forward to working with you."

Then Coach Blevins announced, "After warm-ups, the girls and boys will meet back here for some friendly competition. All right? Good luck, everybody. Let's go!"

J.J. and Hunter were the first to let out a rousing whoop, as the girls and boys split into groups. Team spirit was already at a roaring high, as everyone cheered, yelled, and gave each other high fives.

The girls got right to work warming up their muscles and stretching their tendons and ligaments for a vigorous morning of running. Miss Jablonski showed the girls lots of good stretch exercises to make them as flexible as possible. Then she instructed them to run laps around the school grounds until her whistle sounded.

After the workout, Cassie's hamstrings felt especially limber as she ran with J.J. and Missy Foster. She was pleased to notice that she could keep perfect stride with J.J. today. In fact, Cassie wasn't even panting hard! Missy was keeping up well too, but she was breathing a little more heavily.

"Look alive," said J.J., as they rounded the building to complete their first lap. "Coach Blevins and Miss Jablonski are looking our way!"

"Oh, look," said Cassie, excitedly, "Coach is writing something down on his clipboard about us."

"I hope it's good," said Missy, as she gingerly sprang off the sidewalk and into the grass.

"Me too," Cassie and J.J. replied at the same time. Then all three girls laughed and kept running with more zeal than ever. Even when Miss Jablonski and Coach Blevins sounded their whistles, Cassie felt she could have kept running. She had never felt this loose and energetic after a workout.

After a quick water break, it was time for relays. Coach Blevins assigned some boys and girls to each of two teams—Team A and Team B. Cassie was glad she was on Team A with Hunter and Missy. She only wished she and J.J. could have been on the same team too. J.J. smiled at her from the opposing team huddle and gave her a thumbs-up sign.

Then the teams assembled for the first relay. Iggy lined up and playfully teased his opponents on the other team. His green eyes seemed to laugh as he yelled, "Hey, prepare to lose!"

Tell the Truth, Cassie

"Prepare yourself!" retorted Hunter with a grin. Then to his teammates he said, "All right, we can do this, Team A. Is everybody ready?"

"Yeah!" responded Team A.

Cassie felt a tingle dance through her body, as her excitement bubbled. She was second in line, right behind Hunter. Coach Blevins handed Hunter a baton to carry during the relay run. J.J. would be racing against Hunter, so she got the other baton.

Cassie looked across to see whom she would be running against—Iggy Potts! She tried not to think how long Iggy's lanky legs were next to her shorter ones! Hunter seemed to read her mind. "Don't focus on Iggy. When I hand you the baton, just think about getting to the mark and back as fast as you can. I've seen you run, Cassie. You'll do fine."

"Okay, thanks," she said. Hunter was right. Cassie had to forget everything else and just run. She wouldn't think about competing against Iggy. She would just try to run her very fastest. And when she got back to the starting line, she would hand the baton to—to whom? She looked behind her to see. Oh, of course. It was Missy Foster.

With her short, brown hair wisping about her cheeks in the fall breeze, Missy smiled at her. "I'll be cheering for you. You'll do great," she said.

"I hope so," said Cassie. "I'll cheer for you too!"

Coach Blevins' whistle sounded loud and long. It

was time for the relay race to begin. "All right, every-body. Heads up for the signal."

Hunter and J.J. got into position. "On your marks," said Coach Blevins, with the whistle poised in front of his lips, "Ready, set—whrrrrrrr!" The whistle blew loudly and furiously.

Like two lit firecrackers, Hunter and J.J. exploded off the line. A roar of support from their teammates rose into the air and heightened Cassie's excitement. She wanted to root for J.J. as well as Hunter. They were neck and neck heading toward the halfway mark. But she refrained from cheering at all, knowing she would be next to carry the baton. Next! At the thought, Cassie could hardly breathe.

As Hunter and J.J. fought for the lead, Cassie wasn't sure she could handle her jitters. She could only watch and wait for her turn to come. She couldn't let her team down!

Hunter reached his mark and made his way swiftly back toward his teammates. Neither J.J. nor Hunter seemed to care who was ahead of whom. They were just running with all their might, and both of them were doing very well. Cassie swallowed hard, even though her throat was as dry as a desert. She tried to steady herself.

"Focus on the baton," she whispered, as those around her screamed wildly. She flexed her left hand, which would receive the baton from Hunter. Her leg muscles tightened. She fought to keep them limber and ready to spring into action.

Then a hundred doubts and questions began to flood her mind. What if she stumbled off the starting line? What if she dropped the baton? What if Iggy beat her off the line?

But there was no time to think. Hunter was so near now that she could hear his breathing above her cheering teammates. Her own heartbeat pounded in her ears. Getting a solid footing on the starting line, she leaned forward as far as she could without tipping over. Her left arm stretched out as tightly as a guitar string. Waiting to receive that baton seemed like an eternity!

Yet, before she could even blink, Cassie felt the baton snap into the palm of her hand. She gripped it with all her might.

"Go, go, go, go, go!" Hunter urged.

Cassie's body sprang into action a split second before J.J. could pass her baton to Iggy. The moment of truth had come!

"Show your stuff, Cassie Marie Holbrook," she told herself. "Run like you've never run before!"

Tell the Truth, Cassie

3

Cassie peeled out toward the white chalk line 60 meters down the track. She didn't dare look to see where Iggy was, in case her legs forgot to move. "Just keep putting one foot in front of the other," she told herself, as she steamed ahead. If she were Jeff's hot new sports car, she'd have been in fifth gear by now.

Her toned body seemed to perform much better than she expected during this race of a lifetime. For Cassie, it was her one chance to prove her abilities to Coach Blevins. She was glad to see that her muscles had trained well enough to motor her to the halfway mark, turn 180 degrees, and still have the strength to run back toward her team.

She caught sight of Missy down the track at the starting line, leaning out for the baton, just as Cassie had done a few moments before. She tried to remember Coach Blevins' instructions about passing the baton to her teammate. It would need to be a perfect pass-off.

Halfway back down the stretch, her sweaty palm ached, as it gripped the red baton like a pecan in a nutcracker. Missy was ready to receive it, so Cassie pulled out all the stops. Her legs had never worked so hard. But Cassie told them to do more—to crank up speed that she didn't know she had—until that very moment.

Her teammates cheered her all the way back with more fervor than ever before. In a magical instant, the baton was passed to Missy. Cassie flew past her team-mates, unable to stop her momentum. She doubled over, gulping air into her lungs. Hunter came back to give her a friendly slap on the back.

"Way to go, Cassie!" he exclaimed. There was a little hint of surprise in his voice, as though he couldn't believe what he had just seen. Then he added, "You just beat the Ig-man!"

"Wha-what?" Cassie panted, looking around. She spotted Iggy, who by now was lying flat on the ground, his chest heaving. Hunter grinned. "You raced against long-legged Iggy Potts, and you beat him by a nose. Come on, let's root Missy home now."

Cassie and Hunter joined the others and cheered for their teammate. Missy stumbled a little on her way back toward the finish line, but regained her control quickly. The race between the two teams stayed neck and neck to the final two runners, between Team A's Luke Evans and Team B's Trevor Quincy.

Like Coach Blevins always said in practice, the passing of the baton could be the difference between a win and a loss. A sloppy pass could add a second or two to the race and be the beginning of the end for a team. Cassie and Hunter watched in dismay as a sloppy pass to Luke made him falter to gain control of the baton before he could start running.

Even though Luke tried to regain the seconds he had lost by turning on the speed, Team B was declared the winner "by a hair." Cassie, Hunter, Missy, and all the others on Team A huddled around Luke to congratulate him on his excellent recovery and to reassure Nathan Boyd who was responsible for the faulty baton pass.

"It could have happened to any of us," said Hunter. "Keep your chin up, Nate!"

The relay race had been so close that Cassie almost felt both teams had won. It was a good feeling. She felt especially pleased about her performance. By far, it was the fastest that Cassie had ever run. *But would it be fast enough to earn her a spot on the track team?* she wondered.

But the waiting would soon be over. In just a few hours, she would know…

* * * * * * * * * * * * * * * * * *

Field events were next on the agenda. J.J.'s and Iggy's long legs became quite an advantage for them as they tried out for the long jump. Hunter excelled in the shot put. At Miss Jablonski's suggestion, Cassie tried the hurdles and did pretty well, knocking over only one hurdle out of ten.

By the time the girls headed for the locker room, Cassie was starting to ache. "Owwww," she complained as she took each step. When they reached the locker room, she sank onto a bench. "Ahhhhhhh," said Cassie with relief.

"You are speaking for all of us," giggled J.J., although she didn't seem to be as sore and stiff as Cassie felt. "It was a good tryout for everybody. I'd hate to be the one to decide who is going to make the team and who will be the alternates."

Cassie hadn't really thought of how hard it would be to select the team members until just then. "Poor Coach Blevins!" she exclaimed. "Can you just imagine having to make all those decisions?"

J.J. nodded as her eyes widened. "What a big job that would be! I wonder if Miss Jablonski will help him make the team assignments?" she wondered aloud.

Missy looked around the locker room and back at the girls. "Some of us won't make it," she said a little sadly. "I wish you both all the best."

"You too, Missy," said Cassie. "You're a true team player. We all did our best out there today."

J.J. pulled off her socks and rubbed her tired feet.

Tell the Truth, Cassie

"I think everybody should make the team, don't you?
Anyway, we'll know in a few hours."

As they said good-bye to Missy and all the other
girls in the locker room, J.J. and Cassie slipped on
light jackets so they wouldn't cool off too quickly.
Then they began walking back toward the Holbrooks'
farm. It was quite a walk from the school, but it
would loosen their stiff muscles.

Cassie pulled a couple of water bottles out of her
bag and handed one to J.J. They sipped on the water
and instantly felt revived. Halfway home, when a
dark cloud started to sprinkle them with a little
shower of rain, they felt even more refreshed. Before
they got too wet, they pulled up their hoods and
stuck their hands in their pockets.

"You were great today in the relay," said J.J. "I was
watching you closely. You were as quick as lightning."

"I was?" Cassie asked in genuine surprise. It felt fast
to her, but she didn't know how it looked to everyone
else! "Tell me the truth now, J.J. Was I really fast?"

"As swift as a rabbit being chased by a hundred
hound dogs," said J.J., raising three fingers. "Scout's
honor."

"Wow," Cassie whispered, adding more loudly, "I
sure hope Coach Blevins noticed."

"Oh," said J.J. mysteriously, "I think he noticed all
right. He was talking to Miss Jablonski about you
while you were racing today."

"He was?" Cassie felt her tummy flutter. "What did he say?"

J.J. giggled. "It was during the race. I couldn't hear what they were saying, but Miss Jablonski pointed at you and said something. Coach Blevins nodded in agreement and wrote something on his chart."

"Wow…" Cassie said. "Oh now I really can't wait until we check that list later this afternoon!"

J.J. thought for a moment. "Whatever will we do with ourselves until it's time to find out who made the team?"

"Chores, chores, chores," Cassie said, faking a groan. "Hey, would you mind helping me clean the stalls in the barn? We can get our horses in out of this rain shower and feed them their supper early. Then we can ask my mother or dad to drive us back to the school to check the track team list at 5:00."

"Sounds like a good plan," said J.J.

As soon as the girls arrived at the farm, they couldn't help laughing to see Chester and Gracie standing at the fence near the barn, waiting to be let in out of the soft rain that was falling. When the horses saw the girls, they ran back and forth, up and down the fencerow, as if to say, "Look at us. We're getting wet! Aren't you going to open the door and let us come inside out of this rain?"

But when the girls walked past them chatting, Chester snorted very loudly, and Gracie whinnied.

J.J. looked back over her shoulder and yelled, "Hold your horses, Gracie!"

Cassie laughed. "That's funny. You just told a horse to hold her horses!"

In a matter of minutes, the stalls were picked clean. J.J. and Cassie didn't seem to mind too much emptying the wheelbarrow out on the manure pile at the edge of the pasture. Then they shoveled fresh-smelling dry wood shavings into another, deeper wheelbarrow and dumped several loads of it inside each stall.

Now the barn smelled of pine and leather—Cassie's favorite aroma.

"We should invent a perfume that smells like this," she said.

J.J. giggled, "What would we call it? Barn in a Bottle?" The girls erupted in laughter as they struggled to open the heavy barn door for Gracie and Chester. The horses nosed their way in and immediately went to their stalls.

When Chester didn't find grain in his bucket, he walked quickly into Gracie's stall before Cassie could stop him. Gracie was nibbling in her bucket of grain. Chester wanted her to share the grain with him.

Gracie's ears went flat against her head. That was her warning signal for Chester to get away from her grain, or he was going to be in big trouble! Chester backed off for a moment, but the tantalizing smell of grain tempted him. He boldly nosed back toward Gracie's bucket. In a flurry of mane and tail, Gracie bit Chester's neck, as he helped himself to her grain.

Before there was an all-out horse war, Cassie quickly filled Chester's bucket with a generous scoop of grain, while J.J. clucked to Chester from outside the stall. Chester heard the grain being poured into his bucket, so he lost interest in Gracie's grain and scurried back to his own stall.

"Whew! That was close," said J.J.

With the horses happily munching their grain and a fresh flake of hay each, Cassie and J.J. wearily walked toward the kitchen.

"Horses sure do eat a lot," said Cassie.

"Speaking of eating," said J.J., "I'm starved!"

As they slipped off their shoes at the door, they could smell Mrs. Holbrook's homemade vegetable soup simmering in the slow cooker. Mr. Holbrook sat at the kitchen table reading his evening paper.

He peered over the tops of his reading glasses from behind the paper "Well now, you two have had a busy day," he began. "How did track go this morning?"

"Great! At least, we think so," said Cassie, as she and J.J. washed their hands in the kitchen sink. She handed J.J. a bowl.

"You should have seen your daughter running the relay race and jumping those hurdles," said J.J. She was already spooning up the hot soup.

Tell the Truth, Cassie

"You girls be sure to get some warm biscuits out of the oven," said Mom, as she wiped off the countertops.

Dad put his paper down for a moment and grinned. "I helped make the biscuits, so you know they're delicious," he said.

"That's right," said Mother. "Dad was a big help with preparing supper, so I told him I would clean up tonight."

Dad winked at his "bride," as he still called Mom after 26 years of marriage. Sometimes it seemed as though their honeymoon had never ended.

Cassie chuckled and grabbed two of the biggest biscuits out of the oven. She passed one of them to J.J, and the girls practically inhaled their soup.

With their mouths full, they explained that they needed a ride back to the school, to see if they had made the track team. Mr. Holbrook volunteered to take them in the pickup truck as soon as they finished eating.

"Oh, we're ready now!" exclaimed Cassie, gobbling down the last of her biscuit.

"My goodness, that was quick," said Mom. "I hope you didn't eat too fast, girls."

"It was delicious. Thank you," said J.J. The girls brought their dishes to the sink and rinsed them. Next, they glanced at the clock. It was 4:50 P.M. With any luck, the list had been posted by now. They slipped on their shoes at the door and dashed to the truck.

Beep! Beep-Beep! Cassie played with the truck's horn to hurry her father from the kitchen. A few moments later, Dad appeared flustered as he hurried to the truck.

"What's the big emergency?" he asked, as he climbed inside the cab and started the engine.

"We're dying to know if we made the team," said J.J. sheepishly. "Sorry we're so impatient."

"Yes, sorry, Dad," giggled Cassie, giving her father's arm a tweak. "We're just so excited!"

Tell the Truth, Cassie

4

As soon as the truck had come to a halt in front of the school, J.J. and Cassie spilled out of the passenger side. They stood on the sidewalk, straining to see if the list had been posted. Cassie couldn't be sure. "You go first," she said, swallowing hard. "I'm too nervous to look."

"Is the list there yet? I can't see it," said J.J.

The girls tiptoed up to the school as if the walkway might break. Suddenly Cassie gasped. "There it is!"

The paper containing the list of new track team members was taped on the inside of the narrow, full-length window next to the doorframe. Just as they began to search the list for their names, another vehicle pulled into the school parking lot. It was Missy!

"Oh, let's wait for Missy!" exclaimed J.J. So Cassie and J.J. turned their heads away from the list until Missy had joined them.

When she got out of the car, she called to J.J. and Cassie, "Are our names all there? Did we make it?"

"I don't know," said J.J. "We were just about to find out."

"Yeah," said Cassie, "we're a little nervous."

"Me too!" said Missy. But boldly, she stepped up to the door and began to run her finger down the list that read, "TRACK TEAM—GIRLS."

Down the alphabet, Missy read the last names on the list. "Graystone" and "Holbrook" were both there! Cassie was about to jump up and down, whoop and holler, and do a little dance; but then she realized something. Missy Foster's name was not there. It was listed on a separate sheet labeled "ALTERNATES." The girls were all silent for a moment.

Then Missy turned and faced J.J. and Cassie. Disappointment was written in her eyes, but she really seemed to mean it when she exclaimed, "Congratulations! You both deserve to be on the team."

"But so did you," said Cassie. She tried to think of some way to comfort Missy, but she couldn't find any words to say.

Finally, J.J. hugged her. "Keep coming to practice, Missy. Maybe Coach Blevins will place you on the team soon."

Missy smiled sadly. "I'll think about it," she said. "Oh, well. See you Monday at school!"

As quickly as she had come, Missy was gone. J.J. started back to the truck, but Cassie said, "Wait! What about the boys?"

Tell the Truth, Cassie

"Oh, you know Hunter made it, even if he is only in the sixth grade. He is as fast as the eighth-graders."

"Yes, there's his name," said Cassie, "but what about Iggy?"

"Here it is in the second column—Potts," J.J. read. "Oh, Cassie, all four of us buddies made it! Isn't that great?"

From the way the girls bounced, skipped, and ran back to the truck, Mr. Holbrook already knew the news was good. But in the midst of their celebration, J.J. and Cassie felt terribly disappointed for Missy… and for the eleven other names that were on the alternates list.

"I don't get it," said Cassie, scrunching her nose, as the three of them headed home. "Everyone who was named an alternate is a very good athlete."

J.J. agreed. "We just have to remember that the alternates list could change. For instance, maybe in a few days or weeks, Missy will come off the alternates list and become a team member."

"Yeah," said Cassie, "but only if somebody named to the track team doesn't show up for practice or a meet, or fails a subject, or something like that."

"You're right," J.J. admitted. "The team members are going to work SO hard to stay on the team. With so many talented students trying out this year, it's really an honor to get named to the track team in the first place. We all know that."

They both realized that Missy might be stuck on the alternates list for fall and maybe even spring season, but they vowed to encourage her to keep up her training.

As soon as the girls came inside the Holbrook kitchen, the phone was ringing. Cassie picked up the receiver.

"Hello? Holbrook residence...."

"What's up, Track Superstar?" asked a familiar voice. Cassie grinned. "Oh hi, Iggy!"

"Say hello to Hunter, too," he said. "We're on the speaker phone at my dad's shop."

"Oh! I'll get on the speaker phone too," said Cassie. She pressed a button on the phone, as J.J. joined her.

"Congratulations!" the girls exclaimed together.

"Hey, you two," said Hunter. The girls could hear Hunter and Iggy slapping each other with a high five. "We just wanted to make sure you heard the good news."

"What good news?" asked Iggy.

The girls laughed. "You know what good news," said Cassie. "We made the track team, of course!"

"Oh, right!" said Iggy. He was always a little absent-minded, which added to his comic behavior.

"Duh!" J.J. teased.

"Yep," said Hunter, "that's the good news I meant. It's great, huh?"

"That reminds me," said Iggy. "When Hunter and I

went up to the school today, Coach Blevins was there, taping the list to the window by the door. He said that he and Miss Jablonski have chosen Hunter and J.J. as co-captains of track and field teams."

J.J.'s eyes grew wide. "Wow! Why me?"

"Because you're a good team leader," said Cassie approving of the choices. "You are both team leaders. Way to go, Hunter!"

Cassie gave J.J. a hug. Being on the track team with her best friends was going to make this school year the very best yet!

Tell the Truth, Cassie

5

Cassie's rooster alarm had a day of rest on Sunday. She was up in plenty of time for worship and Sunday School without having to set it.

The rainy afternoon was a lazy one. She spent lots of time in the barn with Chester. While he and Gracie munched on their hay in their stalls, she sat on her pony's spotted back and hugged his neck. All of the extra training exercise over the past few weeks had made her body tired. So Cassie, usually a night owl, went to bed early Sunday night.

The next time the rooster crowed was Monday, reminding her to get up for school. She arose without much coaxing from the unusual clock…mostly because she remembered that she had made the track team.

Cassie headed into her first period class—pre-algebra. Pre-algebra was J.J.'s favorite class besides art, but it was Cassie's least favorite subject.

Oh well, she reasoned, *at least I can get it over with early in the morning*. Besides, even if she didn't like or understand pre-algebra, she did like the teacher—and the teacher seemed to like her.

She walked by Coach Blevins' desk. She wanted to thank him for selecting her to be on the track team, but she decided not to say anything. That would feel just a wee bit awkward. Besides, Missy Foster was sitting right in front of the coach's desk. She didn't want Missy to overhear and be reminded that she hadn't made the team.

"Good morning, Speedy," said Coach Blevins with a half-grin. Cassie smiled. He must have been referring to her performance in the relay race. He made her tingle with pride!

She sat in her desk, which was right behind J.J.'s. The girls talked while Coach Blevins did his first-thing-every-morning teacher duties. When Coach Blevins called, "Listen up," J.J. spun around to face the whiteboard. The rest of the class came to attention, too.

"All right, we'll check those homework papers now," he told them.

As everyone reached into their book bags and binders to get their completed homework assignments, Cassie sat frozen. She couldn't believe it, but she was pretty sure she had forgotten to do her homework. In fact, she couldn't remember what Coach Blevins had assigned on Friday!

Tell the Truth, Cassie

"What homework?" she whispered to J.J., with one eye on Coach Blevins.

J.J. showed Cassie her paper. "You know, the even problems on page 49."

"Oh," said Cassie. *Those x and y problems were a pain*, she remembered.

"Didn't you do your homework?" asked J.J.

Cassie blushed. "Yeah, sure I did! I just forgot for a minute."

Why had she said that? Cassie knew very well that she had forgotten to do her homework. Her mind raced with panic and guilt. She couldn't think about feeling guilty right now for lying to J.J. She simply couldn't afford to get a zero in Coach Blevins' class! She had to keep her grades up, since she had made the track team.

Maybe, Cassie reasoned, *since we are going to check our answers in class, I'll have time to solve the problems now, if I hurry*. All she had to do was turn to page 49 and quickly do the problems, while Coach was reviewing them. She reached into her book bag for her pre-algebra book.

There were her reading and science books, but no pre-algebra book. Where could it be? In her locker, perhaps? It was too late to go to her locker now to look for it. She had to think of something else.

Cassie looked around her. While no one was looking, she slipped out a piece of blank paper and wrote her name, date, and the homework page number in the top left margin.

As Coach Blevins called on students one at a time from around the room to solve each problem on the whiteboard, Cassie quickly scribbled down their work on her paper. She tried to solve some of them herself, because she didn't want to cheat. She had never cheated before in her life, and she hadn't really wanted to start now. But what choice did she have?

Intently working on number 8 on her paper, Cassie was startled when Coach called on her to solve number 10 next on the whiteboard. "I—uh—I didn't get that one," she said faintly.

"All right, J.J., why don't you help us with this one?" he asked. Meanwhile, he wrote out the problem on the board and handed J.J. the marker to solve it.

Cassie felt sick. Now she had not only cheated by copying off her best friend's homework paper, but she had lied—twice.

She had lied to J.J. about having completed her homework. Then she had lied to Coach Blevins about not "getting" number 10. *Well, I really hadn't "gotten" the answer to that question, had I? I just let Coach Blevins think I had tried to solve number 10 and couldn't. Not such a terrible fib to tell, as fibs go…just a little white one, right?* Cassie rationalized.

She decided to finish what she had started. Now that J.J. was at the front of the class, Cassie could see her best friend's work clearly. J.J.'s neatly written homework was lying on her desk, right before Cassie's eyes, at just the right angle. It was so easy…besides, what were friends for?

"Dear God," Cassie prayed silently, as she copied off J.J.'s paper, "if you let me get away with this, I will do my own homework from now on. Amen."

Having the Lord's blessing on this made her feel a little less guilty. If she hurried, she could copy the next few problems. She knew J.J. would have all the correct answers. Cassie felt wicked for doing it, yet she couldn't risk not knowing the answers if Coach called on her again. Then he would definitely suspect that she hadn't done her homework at all!

Cassie couldn't afford any bad grades. She swallowed hard and began to copy J.J.'s work. "I'll never do this again," she repeated to herself over and over.

By the time Coach Blevins had praised J.J.'s work on problem number 10, Cassie had finished copying all the homework problems and how to solve them. Now she would be prepared if she was called on again.

"Cassie, do you understand number 10 now?" asked Coach Blevins.

"Yes, I think so," said Cassie. She felt her face flush pink, because she had barely even paid attention, since she was so busy copying J.J.'s work.

"Good. How about if you come up here and solve

number 12 for us," said Coach.

Now all the blood ran out of Cassie's face. She felt a little faint knowing how close she had come to disaster, but she managed a smile. Weak-kneed, she made her way to the front of the class with her homework paper. The letters and numbers on the page were scribbled so fast, Cassie was surprised she could read them at all. But they were in fairly orderly lines, just the way J.J. had printed the work on her homework sheet.

Still, to Cassie, the pre-algebra problem itself was just one big confusing jumble of letters and numbers. They didn't make any sense to her at all. However, when she finished solving the problem, and got x=6, Coach Blevins said, "That's exactly right. Does anyone have any questions?"

No one said a word. Everyone in the whole class understood how x equaled 6—everyone except Cassie herself. J.J. had saved the day by doing such a good job on her homework.

"Good work, Speedy," Coach Blevins said, as she slinked back to her seat.

"Way to go," J.J. whispered with a smile, as Cassie walked past. She sank into her desk with a sigh. Poor J.J. was cheering her on as though she had done something wonderful. Little did she know... .

No one had suspected a thing. "Speedy" had gotten away with it. She would get a 100 on her homework assignment, and that was all that mattered...wasn't it?

She tried not to think about it anymore. But as Missy Foster demonstrated how to solve number 14, Cassie was never so glad to hear a school bell ring in her life.

"Before you go, here's your homework assignment for tomorrow." Coach Blevins said, as he wrote the page number and problem numbers on the whiteboard. "Now pass your papers to the front of the row and have a nice day," he called over the rustle of bags, books, and papers, as the students prepared to change classes. Cassie passed her homework sheet to the front and was out the door in a flash.

Somehow getting away from there might make her feel less like a criminal, she thought. She also wanted to make sure that her pre-algebra book was in her locker, since she had a homework assignment for tomorrow.

J.J. called after her. "Cassie! Where are you going in such a hurry?"

"Oh," said Cassie, waiting on her friend. "Sorry, I didn't mean to leave you behind! I'm going to stop by my locker before I go to my next class period."

"Coach Blevins is right," said J.J. with her sunny giggle. "You really are Speedy these days! Well, I've got to head in the opposite direction. We're painting our pottery in art today. See ya!"

Opening her locker, Cassie looked high and low for

her pre-algebra book. Under papers, behind her jacket, in the overhead cubby…the book was nowhere to be found. Cassie sighed. "It must be at home, then," she said aloud. But where at home? She had no idea.

For the rest of the day, Cassie felt as though she was in la-la-land. She didn't even feel like sitting with Iggy, Hunter, and J.J. at lunch. She made up an excuse that she wasn't feeling too well and sat alone…well, alone between some eighth-graders she didn't even know. They were acting as though Cassie was invisible, but that was fine with her. She wanted to disappear.

In her mind, she searched for the pre-algebra book in the farmhouse. Or it might have been in Dad's pickup truck. He had brought her to school today. She would need to check there. And of course, it might be in the kitchen, because sometimes she sat at the table and did her studies.

Maybe the missing textbook was in her room, but she was pretty sure it wasn't. She couldn't wait to find it…so that she could do her pre-algebra homework and avoid any more disasters!

As soon as the last bell sounded, Cassie breathed a sigh of relief. Now she could go home and search for her pre-algebra book.

As she walked past the gym, she heard Coach Blevins call, "Hey, Speedy! Where are you going?" She turned around, and there he was with a big grin on his face. "Have you forgotten our track practice this afternoon?"

Cassie felt a cold chill run through her. What was wrong with her? "My goodness," she said, feeling all stuttery and embarrassed. "I guess I'm going the wrong way!" She turned around and headed for the locker room to dress out for track.

By the time practice was over, she was pretty sure she should have skipped track. She should have just headed for home after all. Her timing had been off during the whole practice.

For one thing, she had trouble concentrating. Then, when it was time to relay, she stumbled off the starting line and nearly dropped the baton. Neither Coach Blevins nor Miss Jablonski called her "Speedy" that afternoon!

Before they were dismissed, the girls and boys gathered around Coach Blevins for instructions. Iggy, Hunter, J.J., and Cassie sat down on the bench together as Coach spoke to the group. "I want to give out your schedule of track meets and practices," he said, as he gave them each a copy. It was a very busy schedule—there was either a practice or a meet nearly every day for the next few weeks.

"You will see that our first track meet is coming up on Saturday, and then our second meet will be Tuesday evening. Both meets will be held here at

Misty Falls Middle School."

"Oh, boy," whispered Iggy. "Our first taste of victory—this Saturday!"

"Mustangs rule," whispered Hunter with a smile.

J.J. whispered, "Cass, my mom and your parents are supposed to run the concessions stand Saturday. My mom said she called your mom about it last night."

"Oh, good," said Cassie. "But that means they won't get to see us compete very much. They will be so busy waiting on the crowds."

"They can see us run at the Tuesday meet," said J.J. Cassie nodded and looked away.

"All right, listen up," said Coach Blevins. "I will not be at the meet on Tuesday due to a conflict in my schedule. I will be out of town. Miss Jablonski will be here to coach you. I want you to give her your full attention and cooperation."

"All right, Miss Jablonski," yelled one of the boys. Everyone clapped and whooped for Miss Jablonski, who waved at her fans.

After Coach dismissed them, he walked up behind Cassie as she quickly headed inside. "Tough day?"

"I don't know what was wrong out there," said Cassie, blowing her bangs out of her eyes. Then she smiled confidently. "But don't worry, Coach. I'll work hard and make up for it."

"Spoken like a winner," he quipped. He lightly popped her on the head with his small stack of remaining schedules. "You'll get back on track tomorrow. See you then."

As Coach walked ahead of her, Cassie heard J.J. calling, "Wait up! What's wrong, Cassie? You haven't been yourself all day."

"What do you mean?"

"I don't know. Are you avoiding me?" asked J.J. When Cassie managed to look her in the eyes, she could tell that J.J. felt a little hurt.

"Are you kidding? You're my best friend! Forever, remember?" Cassie said reassuringly.

"Good," J.J. said with relief. "Guess I was worrying for nothing. Hey, did you notice Missy sitting on the bench watching us for a while? I wish she had made the track team too."

Cassie hadn't noticed, but she thought aloud, "Missy could have done a lot better than I did out there today."

"Stop it!" J.J. scolded. "Don't ever put yourself down. You did fine. You can't expect to be 'Speedy' all the time! You just had an off sort of day, that's all! It happens to everybody once in a while."

"Thanks, girlfriend. Are you heading for home?" asked Cassie.

"I was going to walk home with you and help with the horses. Mom said she would pick me up on her way home from work at the children's museum. So we'll have time to work together on our pre-algebra homework, if you like."

"Okay," said Cassie, swallowing hard. If the truth were told, she really just wanted to forget all about that subject. But she couldn't think of anything else, until she found her book.

Maybe if I talk to J.J. about it, I'll feel better, thought Cassie. "I realized in class today that I've misplaced my book. I'm sure it's at home somewhere, though."

"We'll find it," said J.J. cheerfully. "And if we can't, you can look off my book instead."

Cassie felt her face flush again. Little did J.J. know how much looking she had already done that day.

Tell the Truth, Cassie

6

When the girls arrived at the farm, the horses cantered from Possum Creek all the way across the meadow to greet them. The two horses stood inside the fence snorting and nosing at Cassie's and J.J.'s clothes. Gracie's and Chester's eyes seemed to speak that popular message that all spoiled horses ask often: "Got any treats for us?"

"Boy, you can tell they want their grain," giggled J.J. "Why don't I go ahead and feed them? You did all the work this weekend."

"I'll help you," said Cassie. Then on second thought, she added, "Oh, would you mind very much if I try to find my pre-algebra book? It's driving me crazy. I can't think where in the world I left it."

"Sure, go ahead," said J.J. "I'll join you in a bit."

On her way inside, Cassie studied Chester's round middle. "Just a half scoop of grain for Chester. He's getting fat!" J.J. nodded with a giggle.

As she headed indoors, Cassie stopped at the pickup truck to search for her pre-algebra book.

All she found was a little gray mouse that had been disturbed when Cassie looked under the seat. As she squealed, the little creature scampered out of the truck and into the pasture as fast as its tiny feet could go.

There was always something exciting going on at the farm, even if it was just a little mouse surprise. Cassie tried to think of the positive things that had come from stopping by the truck for a look. At least she knew now that her pre-algebra book had to be somewhere in the house, for sure. Secondly, she could ride in the truck knowing that the stowaway mouse was no longer making its nest under the seat!

As Cassie reached the house, she heard Dad's power saw buzzing in his carpentry shop. He had set up his woodworking hobby in a corner of the old barn years ago. She decided to stop by and say hello on her way inside. She could use a hug—the life-sized, teddy bear kind of hug that only her father could give. It had been a rough Monday.

Dad instantly turned off the saw and greeted her. His face and red flannel shirt with holes in the elbows were powdered with fine sawdust. "Munchkin! How was track today?" he asked with true interest.

By the warmth in his eyes, Cassie could tell how proud he was that she had made the team. Many times, she had heard his stories about hurdling in school track meets, when he was known as Hopper Holbrook.

Tell the Truth, Cassie

"Track was not so good today," said Cassie. She hoped he wouldn't be too disappointed in her. "I nearly dropped the baton in the relay."

"Oh, well, that's bound to happen from time to time. Best to just keep your chin up and try again tomorrow," said Dad, as he wrapped his arms around his youngest child. Cassie sank into his saw-dusty embrace and let go of her troubles for a moment.

The smell of the freshly cut wood and her father's gentle touch made her feel so much better. Suddenly she grew curious about the beautiful walnut wood Dad was cutting into measured pieces. "What's this going to be?"

"A country sideboard for your mother. I plan to have it ready for her to serve Christmas dinner on. Don't tell her or your sisters! You know they would let it slip out," said Dad.

Cassie felt special, being entrusted with such a special Christmas gift secret. "Where is Mom right now?" she asked.

"She's at the church decorating her Sunday School room, so I thought I'd slip out here and get all the pieces cut. I selected the wood to match our dining table and chairs."

"Oh, Daddy, you're the best! She will love it." Cassie forgot her troubles and watched her father carefully place the last piece he had cut on the workbench.

Then he lit the old kerosene heater. "It's getting a

little nippy out here. Fall is in the air."

"The coolness feels good to me," said Cassie. "We got really hot today at track practice. But I'd better get inside. Time for homework now."

"Wait a minute," he said. Dad stood up and blew out the match he had used to light the kerosene heater. Then he dropped the smoldering match on the ground and stamped on it with his foot to make sure the flame was completely out. The first lighting of Dad's old faithful kerosene heater was always a sign that Thanksgiving and Christmas were coming.

Dad smiled into his daughter's face. "Cassie, I'm real pleased you're taking your studies so seriously."

Cassie wanted to please him, as she gazed into his eyes. She was glad he was so proud of her.

Then she had another thought....She was also glad that he hadn't seen her cheating off J.J.'s paper earlier today. She was glad he didn't know about her fudging the truth. Suddenly, she felt like dashing into the house, finding her pre-algebra book, and solving every problem in the whole thing to make up for her wicked ways!

She checked the kitchen first for her book. When there was no sign of it anywhere, she grabbed some string cheese out of the fridge to munch on.

Opie was napping in the family room, so she quietly tiptoed upstairs. She didn't need him barking and begging for a tummy-rub right now.

Tell the Truth, Cassie

Pat and Greta weren't in their rooms at the top of the stairs. They must have been at a cheerleading practice tonight. Her older sisters were so busy with school activities that they were hardly ever home.

Cassie began searching her bedroom by lying on her belly for a peek under the bed. When something is lost, look under the bed, was Cassie's motto. All she saw were a few dust bunnies, some scattered Crazy Eights cards, lost dirty socks, her CDs and magazines, and an old crumbly clay model of a cell she had made for science. No pre-algebra book was there.

Next, she stood up and gazed from one end of her room to the other. She hoped to just catch sight of the book. When she glanced at her clean study desk, she recalled raking some items into the drawers that morning.

So she decided to check the drawers. At first, all she saw were a house key and some dusty gym shorts. But digging deeper into the top drawer, aha! She found her book!

Cassie grinned and retrieved it from the messy drawer. "I never thought I'd be glad to see you again," she said.

"Oh no, Cassie's talking to her schoolbooks now. Somebody call the doctor!" teased J.J., as she entered the room and sat on the floor. She slid the backpack off her shoulder and unzipped it. Pulling out her book, she began to work on her math assignment. "Here, these are the problems we have to solve," she said.

Cassie liked studying with J.J., because she didn't waste any time. For some strange reason, J.J. seemed to think homework was fun. Cassie did the first problem by herself. "Did you get x=3 and y=4 for problem number 1?"

"Yes."

"Wow," Cassie bubbled, "I got one right!" She showed J.J. just to make sure she had solved all the steps correctly.

"Good job," said J.J. "See? You can do this. It's like a mystery! You get to solve the mystery with clues. That's why I like math so much. I can't wait until algebra next year."

"Ugh," said Cassie. "I can wait my whole life for that, thank you."

J.J. giggled and finished her work quickly. Cassie was only on problem number 5, as J.J. stored her book and completed homework inside her backpack.

"Are you already done? How did you finish so fast?" asked Cassie. Sometimes it seemed that nothing was hard for J.J. It just wasn't fair.

"Find the fun in it, Cass. You can do it!"

"You sound like Mary Poppins," Cassie said.

J.J. helped Cassie work through problem 5. Amazing! Whenever J.J. helped her, she understood pre-algebra perfectly. Yet when she did homework by herself or on a test, it didn't seem to make sense.

Maybe J.J. was right. Cassie found herself almost having fun solving the final problems. "There. Done. Oh, J.J., you are just the best. You should be a teacher when you grow up."

The girls ran downstairs. In the kitchen, Cassie placed her book in her book bag, along with her homework. She set the book bag by the back door, so that she would be ready to take it to school tomorrow. Now she could relax.

J.J. was leaning over the kitchen sink to peer out the window. Then she said suddenly, "Oh, my mom's here to pick me up. I'll see you tomorrow."

After her friend left, Cassie made a peanut butter and jelly sandwich, poured a glass of milk, and took them to the family room. She turned on her favorite music and sank into the soft sofa. Ah, now this was the life....

Just as she was beginning to "chill out," Mother came in with a box of her Sunday School teaching supplies. "Cassie Marie, please bring your food to the table to eat."

"Oh!" said Cassie with her mouth full. "Sorry, Mom, I forgot. No food in the family room. Don't worry. I didn't spill anything."

She turned off the stereo and took her sandwich and milk to the kitchen table, where her mom began sorting through the supplies. "Our Sunday School room has all new posters up," she said in a teacher-y sort of way. "It's very colorful. I'm going to save these old ones, just in case I want to use them again. They're still in good shape."

Unlike her youngest daughter, Mom was extremely organized, so even the box of old supplies she was finished with was in good order. She never threw anything away, in case it could be recycled.

Lying on the table next to the box was a series of bright-colored small posters. Their purple, gold, and scarlet lettering caught Cassie's eye. The posters looked familiar. They must have been from a series of lessons Mom had taught. She tilted her head to one side so she could examine them.

Oh, of course, now she remembered. She fingered through the posters that listed each of the Ten Commandments in big, fat, funky lettering. She recalled the Sundays that Mom taught about "God's Rules for Life." For ten Sundays straight, Mom had taught about one of the commandments each week until the girls and boys had learned all ten of them.

Cassie remembered that the Lord God had given the commandments to Moses on top of the mountain. It was pretty special how God wanted His children to know how He expected them to live, just like a loving parent. So He had given the commandments to Moses on two big flat rocks called *tablets*.

Tell the Truth, Cassie

How God carved the words right into the stones was beyond Cassie's understanding! She also wondered how Moses had managed to carry the heavy stone tablets all the way down a mountain.

She knew most of the commandments by heart from having a Sunday School teacher for a mom. Let's see, some of them were: "You shall have no other gods before me" and "You shall not misuse the name of the Lord your God," and "Observe the Sabbath day by keeping it holy." That one meant, "don't forget to go to church regularly to worship the Lord."

Cassie pulled out two more posters in the stack, as she finished her sandwich. They read, "You shall not steal" and "You shall not give false testimony."

"You shall not steal" always reminded her of her pesky cousin Petey, who stole a pack of bubble gum one time from the counter at Pepper's Grill when he was just four. Aunt Mary had made him return it and tell the clerk how sorry he was. Petey had pitched a fit and told his mother that he wasn't sorry. He just wanted the bubble gum, but he had to return the gum and apologize anyway.

Cassie stared at the poster that read, "You shall not steal." She tried to think if she had ever stolen anything. Nope, she was pretty sure she hadn't.

Then she read the other poster about "false testimony" once again. Finally she said, "I forget what 'false testimony' means."

"It means anything we say that is not the truth. A lie is false testimony. God is truth, and so He wants us to always tell the truth, to be honest."

"Oh, that's right," said Cassie. "Now I remember."

"Speaking of which, did you clean your room this morning like I asked you to?"

Cassie thought for a moment. "Yes, ma'am," she said, feeling a little twinge of guilt. Mother would not be pleased if she found the drawers in such disarray and things hidden under her bed. But, she reasoned, she had told her mom the truth like the Ten Commandments said. After all, she had spent time cleaning her room that morning, just as she was asked.

"Good girl," said Mother. "Say, would you like these posters for your room on your blank wall? The letters match the colors in your bedspread."

"Okay, maybe I will," said Cassie, accepting the posters as she headed upstairs. "But I won't put them up tonight. I think I'll take a bubble bath and crawl into bed."

"Don't forget to scrub the tub when you get out."

Cassie sighed. Clean my room. Scrub the tub. On second thought, maybe I'll just take a shower.

Tell the Truth, Cassie

7

With J.J.'s help the night before, Cassie scored 100 on her homework. But then she got a surprise when Coach Blevins gave the class a pop quiz with only three problems on it. He said it was to prepare the class for the major test on Friday.

As Cassie worked on each of the problems, she found that she was certain about only one of her answers. She peeked over J.J.'s shoulder just to check her answer on numbers one and three...

"Let's keep our eyes on our own papers," said Coach Blevins as he walked around the room. Cassie looked to see if he was talking to her. His comment seemed to be a general instruction for the class. Whew! That was close.

Cassie decided that she had done the best she could to answer the questions on the quiz. Afterward, Coach Blevins asked everyone to swap papers and grade a neighbor's quiz. J.J. and Cassie swapped papers. Cassie saw right away that two of her answers were different from J.J.'s.

Adventures in Misty Falls

When all was said and done, J.J. had scored 100 on the quiz. But Cassie had a score of $33^1/_3$. Another F.

At least Cassie could proudly show her parents the bright red 100 score on last night's homework paper. After Coach Blevins recorded everyone's scores in his grade book, she tucked the "100-A" homework paper into her backpack.

On the way down the hall to her next class, Cassie wadded up the quiz paper graded F. She slipped it into the trash can. If Mom saw such a grade, she would have a fit and pull her off the track team. But Cassie reasoned that, in a few days, she could bring her grade up, and Mom and Dad would never have to know.

Cassie was a little annoyed with J.J. for writing an F beside 33 and a third anyway. Great. Now her best friend, Miss Smarty Pants, was rubbing salt in the wound.

By the end of the day, Cassie had been assigned three major tests in her classes—all on Friday. The chapter test in reading would be kind of fun. Cassie liked matching and multiple-choice questions in reading—they came easy for her. Then there was another chapter test in science—all essay questions. Ick! And of course, the pre-algebra test. Just to think of studying for all three tests made Cassie's brain feel like spaghetti.

It felt good to run in track practice. Cassie was

back to being Speedy Holbrook. In fact, she jogged all the way home after practice without stopping. She couldn't wait for the first meet on Saturday!

"I'm home!" yelled Cassie as she entered the house. Mmmm...homemade macaroni and cheese was baking in the oven. She drank a full glass of water and looked for signs of life. No one was around, so she went upstairs, with Opie hot on her trail.

In Cassie's room was Mom, on all fours, pulling things out from under her daughter's bed. A dusty cleaning rag was beside her, and her face was flushed red. "I believe I asked you to clean your room, didn't I, Cassie Marie?"

When Cassie's mom called her by her first and middle names, that meant trouble. "Yes, ma'am, I did clean."

"Oh really? Well, let me show you something." Her voice was strained as she opened a dresser drawer and then a study desk drawer. "When I ask you to clean your room, that doesn't mean cram everything into your drawers and closet," she snapped. "You are old enough to clean your room correctly, and I expect you to make an effort to organize this mess before you do anything else."

Cassie didn't know how she would ever explain. But she didn't have a chance to, anyway, because Mom had stormed out and closed the door behind her. With a sigh, she began re-cleaning her room. If only I had cleaned it right the first time. *Ah well, it's too late now*, she thought to herself.

Some of the contents from the drawers went into the trashcan, including the dead batteries and some crumpled, used tissues and a sock without a mate. Progress was rather slow for the first half hour or so, and then Cassie started to see some sparkling results. Her shoes were all lined up in the closet. Pens and pencils were collected from their hiding places all over the room and placed in a cup that said Mustangs Rule! In short, there was a place for everything; and everything, for once, was in its place.

Cassie stood back, sneezed, and admired her work with a sniffle. All that remained was hang the posters of the Ten Commandments. But she would save that for another day. Now she could say in all truth that her room was clean.

With that done, she ran through the kitchen and out to the pasture. Gracie was still grazing in the meadow, but Chester came to greet his owner at the gate. He tossed his head playfully, causing his mane to fly in all directions. Cassie laughed, and before she knew it, she had saddled him.

In a flash, they were off for an evening ride. She wanted to ride and ride right into the setting sun, if she could get that far! The fall breeze refreshed her and soothed her. In the back of her mind, teachers were echoing reminders to study for tests on Friday. She would do that as soon as she finished her ride ....

Chester and Cassie followed Possum Creek all the way to Misty Falls, the cascading waterfall for which their town was named. While Chester took a long drink of water, Cassie spread out on a big boulder that was cool to the touch. She let the mist from the waterfall cool her forehead and cheeks, and she didn't mind that dusk was falling.

When she arrived back at the farm, a full moon served as her flashlight. Gracie was still waiting to be taken into her stall in the new barn. Cassie opened the gate and led Gracie and Chester together into the barn. After horse chores, she was starving and ready for a hot bath.

"Oh, thank goodness you're all right," said Mother as Cassie walked in the door. "I was getting ready to send your dad out with the truck to look for you. Didn't you hear us ring the big bell?"

"I didn't mean to worry you," said Cassie, kissing her mother. "Did you see my room?"

Her mom's face beamed. "Yes, it's much better. Thank you, dear. Now you must be hungry." The oven-baked macaroni with extra cheese really hit the spot.

By the time Cassie had washed her hair and gotten ready for bed, it was bedtime. For a moment, she considered pulling out her books to begin studying for the big tests on Friday. Yet, it was already time for lights out. Maybe she would just sit up in bed and read through her notes from science class.

Before she knew it, she was dozing as Dad leaned over to kiss her goodnight and collect her study notes off the bed. "You'll have to finish tomorrow, Munchkin," he said, switching off the light. "Sleep tight."

Cassie realized as soon as she awoke the next morning that she hadn't finished her homework, but there was no time left to do it. In first period, rather than going over the math problems as usual, Coach Blevins collected the papers right away.

When Cassie didn't turn in homework, Coach Blevins called her up to his desk. "Is everything all right at home?"

"Yes," said Cassie. "Why do you ask?"

"I thought maybe you had a good reason for not doing your homework today," he said, as he wrote a zero in his grade book beside her name. "You realize that you have a couple of zeros in my class now. This is going to affect your overall average. I'm getting concerned that it could threaten your status on the track team."

Cassie sighed and tried to think fast. "I did have a busy night. Uh, our family had special plans. That's why my homework didn't get done."

She felt her face flush, as she tried to think what was so special about eating macaroni and cheese and cleaning her room. (She thought she'd better not mention that she had had time to ride her pony, but not enough time to do her math homework and study for tests.)

"I see," said Coach Blevins, his face more somber than Cassie had ever seen it. "Well, let this serve as a warning, Cassie. You must do well on the major test in pre-algebra this Friday, or I will have to replace you on the track team."

"Yes, sir," she said shakily. "You'll see; I'll ace that test. I'm going to study every spare minute."

With Coach Blevins' warning ringing in her ears all day, she could hardly think of anything else. Running track meant so much to her! She was willing to do just about anything to make sure she retained her spot on the team. Besides that, she wanted to please her parents with good grades, even if it meant tossing a few low grades in the garbage from time to time.

She was glad she had done just that when Mom asked to see her graded papers from all her classes Thursday night. It was the night before three tests, so Cassie was up to her eyeballs in study notes and books. Cassie showed her all the papers she had collected over the past week that were a C+ or above. But she had discarded anything under a C into the trashcan at school.

Fortunately, J.J. had gone straight home after track practice instead of coming over to study with her

after all. J.J. would have known about the missing
papers with F on them from pre-algebra, since she
had graded a couple of them.

As it was, Mom was pleased to see that Cassie was
doing well. At least it appeared that way. And right
now, that was all that mattered at the moment. She
simply couldn't be pulled off the track team, by her
parents or by Coach Blevins. She was finally becom-
ing good at something!

As Mom looked through graded papers in all
Cassie's subjects, she said, "It doesn't appear that you
have many grades for math. Are you sure these are all
there are?" Now she was looking at her daughter
squarely in the eyes.

Cassie felt warm and dizzy. "Yes, ma'am."

Mother handed the stack of papers back to her. "It
looks just fine. Good work, dear," she said, leaning
down to kiss her daughter on top of her head. "Now,
while you're studying, I'd better get down to my
sewing room and finish a project I started for a lady
across town. Oh, there are milk and chocolate chip
cookies for you when you need a study break!"

"Chocolate chip, my favorite!" exclaimed Cassie.
Her mom went downstairs to the basement room,
where she had a sewing business. Meanwhile, Cassie
was glad the twenty questions were over. She was
starting to breathe more easily now.

Here it was—Thursday night, and she was quickly

running out of time to study. This time tomorrow the tests would all be over. She felt confident in reading and pretty confident in science. So she decided to spend all her time going over pre-algebra problems from each section that would be covered on the test. There seemed to be too many rules and formulas to keep up with, and all just to find out what x equals.

Later, when she went out to the barn to tuck the horses in their stalls for the night, she took her pre-algebra with her. She even told Chester and Gracie how to solve for x and y.

All that night, she dreamed of taking her pre-algebra test. The classroom was set up outside on the track and field! Every now and then, Coach Blevins would blow his whistle and say the same thing he had told her just a few days before: "You must do well on the major test in pre-algebra this Friday, or I will have to replace you on the track team." Then Missy would come running onto the field in her track clothes and take the baton from Cassie and run away with it.

The dream occurred over and over, until Cassie awoke to her rooster alarm in a cold sweat on Friday morning. She had not rested well that night. All she wanted now was to have her tests over.

The math test was two pages long with 40 problems on it. She was clipping along at an easy pace until she hit number 10. She was pretty sure she had gotten

the answer correct, but she wanted to be sure. J.J.
was deeply involved in solving the problems on her
test. Cassie checked to see if Coach Blevins was looking. Since he was working on some papers, she felt
free to try to compare her answer with J.J.'s. So she
scooted as far left in her seat as she could without
falling in the floor. Then she managed a peek.

Sure enough, she had the same answer J.J. did!
Pleased with herself, Cassie continued to work.
Numbers 11-15 were simple to solve. But 16-20 were
really hard for her. When J.J. got up to sharpen her
pencil, Cassie quickly copied her friend's answers
onto her own paper. She was desperate to do well, to
keep her place on the track team ....

In the last ten minutes of class, Cassie still had quite
a few problems to finish. She was sure that she would
run out of time. She could tell that J.J. had completed
her test paper and was just checking her answers. By
now, Coach Blevins was walking around the room to
see how the students were coming along. When his
back was turned, Cassie looked beyond J.J.'s long
dark hair and captured a few more answers for her
test paper.

By the time the bell rang, Cassie had an answer for
every problem except one. She was pretty sure she
had made at least a B if not an A. With a sigh of
relief, she wrote her name at the top and turned in

her test paper.

"How'd we do, Speedy?" asked Coach Blevins, accepting her test.

"I think I did pretty well," said Cassie with a smile. "When will you have the tests graded?"

"Probably not until Monday," he said. Then he winked. "See you at the track meet tomorrow."

Cassie smiled. Home free at last. She felt so light and free that she floated out of the room. Finally, the hard part was over; and she knew she had gotten at least most of the right answers, thanks to J.J.

"Cassie!" J.J. called from behind, as Cassie sped down the hall. "Where are you going again in such a hurry? My goodness, you are Speedy, all right."

J.J. wasn't really the person she wanted to talk to right now. It was hard to look her friend in those soft, midnight blue eyes after just cheating off her paper.

"Can you believe it? I have another test to take! Gotta run!" Cassie called over her shoulder. She left J.J. standing in the hall looking confused and bewildered, but she just couldn't talk to her. Not now.

Tell the Truth, Cassie

8

Saturday's track meet was spectacular. With the tests successfully out of the way, Cassie was relaxed and ran her very best time yet. She worked hard at the relay events and helped make up some time for the Mustangs. She hurdled; she sprinted; she cheered for her teammates. They won their first track meet by more than a few points! Missy Foster was one of the few alternates who were there to watch from the sidelines.

Although Mr. and Mrs. Holbrook and Ms. Graystone were working in the concessions stand, Cassie could hear them cheering in the distance. There was no mistaking Dad's high-pitched bird-call whistle, or Mom's "That's my girl!" cheer. Cassie looked forward to Tuesday night's meet, when they would actually be sitting in the stands, better able to watch her every move.

As Cassie sat down on the sidelines with Hunter and Iggy and J.J. to drink her limeade that her parents had provided for the team, Coach Blevins walked to the concessions stand. As he bought a soda, he talked for a moment with Cassie's parents. She could see them smiling and talking and then listening to Coach. Cassie knew they must have been talking about her improvements in track. She smiled to herself with satisfaction.

Then a horrible thought occurred to her. She wondered if the conversation had turned to the subject of pre-algebra? *Of course not*, she thought, *that's impossible*. Since Cassie knew she had scored well on the test Friday, she wasn't worried…not too worried. *No, I'm not going to worry at all*, she decided.

Cassie even talked and cut up with J.J. on the way to the locker room. Maybe now she should work on resuming her close friendship with J.J., but J.J. seemed a little cool toward her.

The next day after church and Sunday dinner, Pat, Greta, Jeff, and even Opie were all excused with Dad to hike along Possum Creek to Misty Falls. Cassie wanted to go too, but Mom had asked her to help wash dishes.

Reluctantly, she stayed behind. At first Mom was quiet. Then she said, "I was proud of you for your performance yesterday at the track meet, Cassie Marie."

Cassie Marie? Mother usually used her whole name when she was upset about something. But this time, she was talking about the track meet. That was a good thing, wasn't it?

Tell the Truth, Cassie

"Thanks! I can't wait for you to see us Tuesday night. Our team is going to be awesome this year. Don't you think?"

"It appears that way," said Mother. "Coach Blevins is very impressed with your ability. He came by the concessions stand to tell us so."

"He is? He did? Oh tell me, what did he say?"

"Well," said Mother, "your endurance level has been improving. He called you 'Speedy' too."

Cassie giggled. "Yes, he's been calling me that since the tryouts. That's when I really tried to turn on the speed, and he noticed!"

"Is everything else all right at school, dear?" Mom asked suddenly.

Cassie looked at her, a little alarmed. "Sure, why do you ask?"

"Oh nothing. I just wanted to be certain that we're being honest with each other."

Cassie swallowed hard and smiled weakly. She didn't like where this was going. Did Mom know something she wasn't sharing? "Everything is loaded in the dishwasher. Could I try to catch up with Dad and the Holbrook gang now?"

"Go ahead, dear. I'll stay here and maybe catch a nap."

Cassie kissed her mom and went to slip on her old walking shoes. As quick as a gazelle, she ran across the pasture toward Possum Creek. Dad's cattle in the next field over "mooed" at her.

When Chester came trotting along beside her, Cassie slipped onto his bare back like J.J. had taught her. Chester wasn't wearing a bit, so there were no reins to steer his head. Yet her pony knew where she wanted to go.

He was hot on the trail of the Holbrook family. Cassie could see their footprints along the creek bank. As she rode along at a fast walk, she wished J.J. could be there just now.

She missed her friend, who hadn't been around much this week. But since Cassie had looked on J.J.'s papers, she felt ashamed. Suddenly she realized how much J.J. trusted her, and how much she trusted J.J. She was sorry that she had broken J.J.'s trust. Her friend must never know about that, and Cassie promised herself never to cheat again ....

Cassie caught up with Jeff, Pat, Greta, and Dad at Misty Falls. They were sitting on the big boulder in front of the falls, letting the fine mist dance on their faces.

"Come on over, Sis," yelled Greta, patting a spot on the rock next to her.

Cassie slid off Chester's back and hopped rocks to the place where they were assembled. Dad appeared to be asleep. But when she sat down, he tickled Cassie's tummy.

She loved her family so much. She knew it was quite unusual for a family with so many brothers and

Tell the Truth, Cassie

sisters to get along as well as they did. Sometimes she missed her brother Sid, who was grown up now. And here, at Misty Falls, was the best place in the world to be a girl with her whole life and all of her dreams ahead of her.

Cassie laughed at her brother, who wibble-wobbled on Chester's back as they headed back toward the Holbrook farm. "See y'all back at the ranch," he called, adding a yippy-yi-yay just for fun.

As Greta and Pat hopped more stones along the creek bed, Dad whispered to Cassie. "Would you like to help me in the old barn with the secret Christmas project for your mama?" he asked.

"Sure!" she said. "I'll just get my other shoes upstairs and meet you in the woodworking shop."

When Cassie arrived in her room, Mom was there tacking up the last of the Ten Commandments posters. Each poster was turned at a different angle to make sort of a Ten Commandments collage. "That looks great! Thank you!" exclaimed Cassie.

"You're welcome," she said softly. "Did you have a nice walk?"

"Yes, we hiked all the way to Misty Falls and back. Chester hauled Jeff all the way home without a bridle on," giggled Cassie. "You should have seen him. He nearly fell off several times."

"I'm glad you had fun," said Mom, with a smile. Then she yawned. "Now I'm really off for my nap."

As Cassie closed the door, she thought her mom was acting a little too reserved or quiet or something. Perhaps she was just tired.

The posters looked great, and she read each of them again as she got dressed:

You shall have no other gods before me.
You shall not make idols.
You shall not misuse the name of the Lord your God.
Observe the Sabbath day by keeping it holy.
Honor your father and mother.
You shall not murder.
You shall not commit adultery.
You shall not steal.
You shall not give false testimony.
You shall not covet (desire what belongs to someone else).

As soon as Cassie had changed into her other shoes, she dashed to the barn. She was pleased that Dad had asked for her help. It was kind of special working with him in secret to build a special surprise for Mom—especially when her Jeff and the girls didn't know anything about it.

"What can I do to help?" she asked as she entered the work area.

Dad's hair was still damp from the mist at the waterfalls, and he lit the kerosene heater. "This will knock the chill off," he said. "How about if you sand each of those cut pieces to get the rough edges off?"

"Okay," said Cassie. For the next half hour, she sanded each piece of Mom's future country sideboard with the sandpaper—first with the rough side, then with the finer sand side.

"Your job is very important," said Dad. "You're removing all the unwanted splinters that make the wood rough."

"I'm trying really hard to make the wood very smooth to the touch," said Cassie. "Feel it right here." She took her father's hand and ran it along the wood where she had been working.

"Very smooth," said Dad. "You know, sometimes when we choose to do the wrong thing, our sinful choice makes us rough like this piece of wood."

"I never thought of it that way," said Cassie. Then she added, "I guess God has to sand away our sin and make us smooth too!"

"That's what life is all about," said Dad. "God is perfecting us, just like you are perfecting that piece of wood that will make your Mom a beautiful country sideboard."

Cassie didn't feel like God was sandpapering her. Was He? "Dad, how is God smoothing out my rough edges?"

Dad reached for his measuring tape and a pencil. As he marked the wood where a notch would be cut, he said, "Oh, He takes His time and lets us learn hard lessons from the things we experience."

"What things?" Cassie asked.

"Oh things about life, important lessons, like about doing your best, and being honest, and things like that."

"Oh," said Cassie. "Dad, do you suppose that God cares if we tell a little bitty lie once in a while?"

"Why, I suspect He does," said Dad. "I suspect He wants His children to tell the truth all the time, because He stands for the truth."

Cassie sanded the wood harder, so hard that her arm got tired. When she was finished, the piece was perfectly sanded and ready to become the countertop for Mom's new country sideboard.

She watched Dad bevel a pretty border into the wood. Woodworking took a long time and a lot of labor. At dusk, the sideboard was beginning to take shape, but there were many steps in the process to finish. Dad and Cassie had really just begun.

As they cleaned up and got ready to go inside, Cassie asked if she could turn off the kerosene heater. It was a treat to get to control the flame as it died out. "Sure," said Dad. "Be sure to turn the knob all the way to the left."

"Okay," said Cassie. "I remember."

A little later, Cassie checked through her book bag and made sure she had everything ready for school the next day. This time, she didn't have any home-work, since all her major tests were Friday. Her teach-ers had given their students the weekend off.

On Monday in pre-algebra, Coach Blevins handed back their graded test papers. He announced that no one had made a 100, but that J.J. Graystone had come very close with a 96. Cassie applauded her friend with the rest of the class.

If J.J. had done well, then Cassie must have received a good score too. Sure enough, Cassie scored a 90! It was barely an A. Still, it was an A! Coach Blevins would certainly let her keep her place on the track team now!

"Way to go, Cassie! I knew you could do it!" exclaimed J.J. She was her old warm, friendly self.

"Thanks for those times you helped me understand how to do the problems better," said Cassie a little weakly.

"What are best friends for?" J.J. reminded her.

After class, Coach asked Cassie to stay after the bell had rung. Perhaps he wanted to congratulate her. But he had something else in mind ....

"I asked you to stay, because I want to ask you a very important question, and I would appreciate the truth," he began.

Cassie gulped and felt her face run hot.

"Were the answers on the test Friday your own answers?"

Cassie blinked at Coach Blevins. "Yes, sir," she said. *After all*, she reasoned, *I put the answers on the paper myself; no one else wrote on my paper.*

Coach Blevins stalled for a moment and cleared his throat. "Cassie, did your eyes stay on your own paper the entire time you were working?"

She wanted to say yes. But she didn't want to lie altogether. "I might have looked up a few times to collect my thoughts," she said, satisfied that she was still mostly telling the truth.

"Well now, I'll tell you why I am asking," said Coach Blevins. "I found it odd that you and J.J. had both gotten the same wrong answer on two of the questions. Those wrong answers were careless mistakes on J.J.'s part. She had shown her work on her paper, but there was no work shown on your test paper. I just wondered how you arrived at the very same wrong answers."

Cassie shifted her weight from one foot to the other. Her breathing got a little faster. "I don't know, Coach," she said. "It was just one of those weird things, I guess."

Coach Blevins sighed and looked a little disappointed. "I'm going to be straight with you, Cassie. I am 99 percent sure I saw you cheating off J.J.'s test paper Friday. But I'm going to give you the benefit of the doubt. You can remain on the track team, but as of right now, you are on probation."

Tell the Truth, Cassie

"Probation? What do you mean, Coach?"

"I mean one more thing happens—failure to turn in homework, cheating, anything, and you're off the team. Remember that as a member of the Misty Falls Middle School track team, you are to set a positive example for others, Cassie. I'm hoping that you didn't cheat Friday. I'm trusting that you didn't. I want to believe you, Cassie."

Cassie didn't know what to say. She looked at her shoes to hide the tears welling in her eyes.

"This is just between us, and it never has to leave this room, all right? Don't let the team down. But more importantly, don't let yourself down."

"Yes, sir," said Cassie, almost in a whisper. Suddenly, she wasn't so proud of her test with the 90-A written in red across the top. Cassie felt about two inches tall as she walked out of Coach Blevins' class.

Is that why Mom had posted the Ten Commandments on her wall and was acting strangely over the weekend? Had Dad said those things in the old barn about sin because she was suspected of doing something wrong? Hadn't Coach Blevins told her this was between the two of them, and no one had to know?

How had she gotten herself into such a mess?

Tell the Truth, Cassie

9

That night, Mother asked to see Cassie's graded test paper in pre-algebra. She also asked for science and reading, but those tests hadn't been returned yet. Besides, Cassie was sure she had done fine on those.

Trying to hide her guilt from Mom was really hard, but Cassie gave her smile an extra-wide effort as she presented the 90-A test score. Her mom did seem very pleased, and she praised her for doing such a good job.

Then she asked, "Did you ever get back any more homework papers from Coach Blevins?"

"No, I don't think so," said Cassie. She tried to forget that she had thrown away a couple of poor grades. She tried to forget that she had received a zero for failing to turn in homework.

Mother was looking at her intently. "Oh, I see," she said. "Well, congratulations again on the good test score. I believe after the track meet tomorrow, I'll just have a word with Coach Blevins and make sure all your work is satisfactory."

Cassie glared at her mother in horror. "Why would you do that? I told you everything. Besides, Coach Blevins won't be at the track meet tomorrow. Miss Jablonski will be in charge. Coach Blevins said he would be out of town."

"Oh?" said Mother. "It must be very important for him to miss a track meet. Well, never mind. I'll just give him a call at school on Wednesday."

"B-b-but," Cassie stammered. She had to keep Mom from talking to Coach Blevins until some time had gone by...until the dust had settled...until she could prove herself to Coach Blevins again.

"But what?" asked Mom.

"He-He's had a death in his family," she said finally, with her fingers crossed behind her back. "I think he will be out of school for the rest of the week. It was his father, you know."

"Oh dear," said Mother. "What a shame. You know what we should do? Bake his family some cookies. Perhaps some of your delicious snickerdoodles."

"But he won't be here to eat them," said Cassie. "He will be at the funeral."

"Oh? And where is the funeral? Did he say?"

"I'm not sure, but I think it is California," said Cassie. She couldn't believe how the lies kept rolling off her tongue.

Oh well, at least Cassie had success in discouraging Mom from talking to Coach Blevins this week. She dropped the whole thing. Cassie was shaking all over from the stress—it took a lot of effort to make up tall tales.

The next day, Cassie expected to have a substitute teacher in pre-algebra. But there was Coach Blevins behind his desk as always!

She leaned forward and whispered to J.J. "I thought Coach wasn't going to be at the meet tonight?"

"Oh, he's not," said J.J. "There's a meeting this afternoon in downtown Atlanta. I heard him telling Miss Jablonski about it. He said he wouldn't be back for the track meet."

"Oh," said Cassie, trying not to look too relieved. She tried to pretend that nothing was out of the ordinary.

"Are you okay?" J.J. asked suddenly. "You look a little pale."

"Fine! I'm fine," Cassie assured her.

"Hey, guess what? Missy Foster is going to dress out with the team at tonight's meet! Isn't that great news?" J.J. said excitedly.

"Why? I mean, sure that's great! But is someone dropping off the team?" asked Cassie.

"Not that I know of," said J.J. "I guess Coach just wants her talent. She hasn't missed a single practice, you know. She's getting better all the time."

That afternoon in reading class, Cassie glanced out the window just in time to see Coach Blevins leaving the school in his sports car. What a relief! Now that he was really gone and Mom wouldn't bump into him tonight, Cassie could begin to relax.

After school, she dashed home to take care of the horses, have a quick bite of supper, and change into her track clothes. Dad worked in the old barn until nearly time to go to the meet.

When he came in for supper, he asked Cassie to run out and turn off the kerosene heater. "I left it on by accident, Munchkin. Just make sure that you turn the knob—"

"I know," said Cassie, "all the way to the left! I'll turn it off for you."

Cassie ran out to the old barn. But on her way, she noticed that Chester had gotten out of his stall and was wandering around the yard, munching green grass.

"Hey! How did you get out, Mister?" Cassie whopped his backside with her hand and guided him back to his stall. She glanced at the clock and realized that the track meet started within 20 minutes. She had to get to the school now!

She hurried inside and told her parents it was time to leave. "All right," said Dad, "I'm just finishing up here. Let's roll!"

The three of them had hopped into the truck and were halfway to the school when Dad asked, "Are you sure you turned off the kerosene heater in the old barn?"

Cassie's heart skipped a beat. She couldn't believe she had forgotten to turn it off. It was Chester's fault for escaping. But it was too late to turn around and go home now, or she would be marked late. Cassie was already on probation. She couldn't risk being late!

"I turned it off," said Cassie. Inwardly, she promised herself that she would sneak into the old barn and turn off the heater as soon as they got home.

"That's my girl," said Dad, patting her knee. "Speedy Holbrook!"

"It's such a shame about Coach Blevins's father," said Mom. "Did you hear about that, Joe?"

"You told me at the house," said Dad. "I'm really sorry to hear about it. Coach Blevins must be pretty torn up, losing his father like that."

"We'll sure miss him tonight," said Cassie. She couldn't wait to get out of the truck when they reached the school.

"Go get 'em!" yelled Dad after her. Cassie waved back to him and dashed into the locker room.

When the girls ran down the hill with the rest of the team for the meet, there stood Coach Blevins with Miss Jablonski. He didn't look one bit sad, as though he could have lost a family member. He was laughing and talking to Miss Jablonski and the school principal!

What was Coach doing here? she wondered. Didn't he know that his father had died in California and that

Mom was going to deck him with a bunch of cookies if he didn't leave town? Or at the very least, didn't he have a meeting in Atlanta?

Cassie felt the blood draining from her body and into her feet. She thought she might faint, as Missy sat down next to Cassie and J.J.

When everyone had gathered, Coach called the roll and gave his usual pep talk. Cassie spotted her mom and dad in the stands, as she sort of overheard J.J. ask, "So, Coach, did your meeting get out early?"

"Sure did," said Coach. "And boy am I glad! I didn't want to have to miss this meet. The visiting team is one of the toughest in our district. We always have a tight competition with them, but we can beat them this year. Just get out there and be the boys' and girls' teams I know you can be!" There was a roaring cheer from the Misty Falls Mustangs. They were ready for action. Everyone except Cassie, that is, who was in a daze.

She could just imagine what Mom would say to Coach if she got half a chance...how sorry she was to hear that he had lost his father, how bravely he was handling it, and when was he leaving for the funeral in California? Then Coach Blevins would look confused and say there was no death in his family...and why would he go to California for a funeral and how did she ever come up with such a cockamamie story....

"Calm down," Cassie told herself, as she breathed

deeply. She decided that what she had to do right now was run her best time yet to remain on the team…and somehow keep Mom and Dad from talking at all with Coach Blevins…or she would be a cream puff on a cracker later tonight.

"Dear God," Cassie prayed, as she realized that this was getting out of hand, "please help me out of this mess. Help me to run like the wind tonight! In Jesus' name, amen."

During the first relay run, Coach Blevins stood nearby as the referee aimed the starting gun in the air. "On your marks …."

Cassie glanced into the stands to see her parents standing in support of her.

"Get set…pop!" The gun fired.

Cassie shot off the line as the starting runner. Like never before she tore down the stretch to the mark and pivoted perfectly to return to the starting line. With the baton poised in her hand, Cassie prepared to pass off to Missy.

But when her foot came down, it twisted on the landing. She recovered in time to cross the finish line ahead of the competition, successfully passing the baton, but pain was shooting through her left foot.

For the rest of the night, Cassie sat on the sidelines, with a big bag of ice on her foot. The team doctor said it was just a mild sprain, but that she should stay off of it for a couple of weeks. Missy took her place in the hurdles, the remaining relays, and sprints. What else could possibly go wrong tonight?

The only good thing that came out of Cassie's foot injury was that Mom didn't get a chance to talk to Coach Blevins. They came out of the stands to take Cassie home right after the last event. Dad drove his truck right down to the track so that she wouldn't have to hobble up the long hill.

As everyone cheered the victory for the home team, Coach Blevins and Miss Jablonski were mobbed by excited parents and students. As Mom helped Cassie into the truck, J.J. asked for a ride to their house. "I want to check on Gracie," she said. "Besides, my buddy sprained her ankle. She needs me!"

It was a tight fit, but everyone piled into the truck. Driving out of the crowded parking lot, Mother said, "What a shame about Coach Blevins' father. Did you see all those people gathering around to give him their sympathies? How brave he was to come to the meet tonight! Now that is true dedication!"

"Sympathies? What?" asked J.J., scrunching up her nose. "What happened to Coach Blevins' father? "

"Never mind," said Cassie. "I'll tell you later."

From a good distance away, Cassie noticed that a strange black rain cloud seemed to hang low in the sky over the Holbrooks' farm as they approached. Then an orange-red light glowed out of its blackness. Suddenly, Dad sped up the truck.

Tell the Truth, Cassie

"Joe, what's the matter?" asked Mother.

"Fire!" exclaimed Dad.

Cassie rose up for a better look. It was the old barn! In an instant, she knew but didn't want to believe it. Dad's old faithful kerosene heater—the one she hadn't turned off before her track meet—

Dad turned on his wireless phone and instantly called 911—"Fire!" he exclaimed, in an alarming tone. "Hurry! The Holbrook Farm!"

10

At a safe distance, Dad parked the truck and ran for the water hose at the house. He directed the stream of water toward the angry flames. The fire was already working its way through the corner of the old barn, where Dad's woodworking shop was located.

In the autumn breeze, smoke billowed and blew into the new barn. As Cassie and J.J. got out of the truck, they could hear the horses whinnying. Chester! Gracie!

As J.J. ran full throttle to get Gracie out of the new barn, Cassie followed as quickly as her injured foot would let her. There was no fire in the new barn, but the smoke was thick and toxic.

Dad called, "Stop, girls! Let the firemen get the horses out."

J.J. stopped, dropped to her knees and began to sob. "Gracie, oh Gracie! Poor Chester!"

Opie was barking at the back door of the house. The barn cats were huddled together on the front porch of the Holbrook house. Cassie felt numb.

Firefighters arrived at the Holbrook farm. Two of them crawled underneath the billowing smoke that blew in and around the new barn. In a few minutes that seemed like hours, Gracie and then Chester flew at a gallop toward safety in the pasture. Cassie was there at the gate to let them in.

Cassie caught sight of her father, as he watched helplessly as the firefighters worked. His question rang in her ears, "Munchkin, did you turn off the kerosene heater?"

Now Cassie had to face what she had caused. This was her fault. Now the tears could flow. She could no longer bear to watch.

She hobbled up the stairs and into her room, falling on the bed and sobbing her heart out. Suddenly she realized the truth of all that had happened. Her little tiny lies had grown to become great big monsters that were now swallowing her whole, and even causing harm to those she loved most.

Cassie's face was as swollen as a jellyfish, by the time she tried to stop crying. But when she read, "You shall not give false testimony," posted on her wall, she started crying all over again.

There was a knock at her door. It was J.J. "The fire is under control," she said. "The old barn is the only building that got burned—but only partly. May I come in?"

Cassie was relieved the fire was out, but it didn't

quench the sorrow in her heart. "Oh, J.J.," she said, "You probably never want to come over here ever again."

"Why would you say that?" asked J.J., handing Cassie a box of tissues.

"Because I caused this fire. I told my father that I had turned off the kerosene heater, when I knew that I hadn't. I lied, because we were going to be late for the track meet. I was selfish, and look what almost happened. Chester and Gracie could have been killed! My house could have burned down!"

J.J. sat on the bed next to Cassie. "But the worst didn't happen, Cassie. God didn't let the worst happen. You're my friend, Cassie Holbrook. No matter what, you're my best friend. I love you. Everything is going to be okay."

"No it isn't. You wouldn't say that if you knew that I cheated on my math test and some homework papers by looking at your work," said Cassie. She almost wanted J.J. to be angry with her. It would make her feel better, somehow.

But J.J. wasn't angry. She was terribly disappointed, but not angry. It would have been easier for Cassie to take if J.J. had been angry. But to have her best friend in the world disappointed in her—well, that was just the worst!

"I wouldn't blame you if you never trusted me again," said Cassie, sniffling horribly.

"Oh, Cassie, God must have allowed this fire tonight to teach you something," J.J. whispered. "Don't you see? He let the barn catch fire to get your attention, so that you would stop cheating and stop lying and only tell the truth from now on!"

Cassie hadn't thought of that. But it did make sense. She was sure she would never tell another lie. And if she did, she would remember the old barn fire, take back the lie, and tell the truth instead.

Suddenly, in the midst of her tears, Cassie began to laugh. Right then she promised God and J.J. that she would always tell the truth, even if the truth hurt.

She had to get downstairs. Dad and Mom must know right away what she had done, even if she were to be punished for the rest of the school year—or the rest of her life! They deserved to know the truth.

When Cassie limped outside with J.J.'s support, Mom and Dad were talking to the chief firefighter. Jeff, Greta, and Pat were home now too, and they were huddled around the firefighter to hear what he had to say.

"The blaze destroyed only part of the barn, Mr. and Mrs. Holbrook. It was the part where the woodworking shop was set up. Unfortunately, most everything in that area was destroyed."

Mom's Christmas present! Dad's tools! Gone! Cassie began to cry anew. But she couldn't wait another second to confess. Her heart was heavy and so very sad. She was so sorry for what she had done.

She confessed to her parents with bitter tears, "I was responsible for the fire. I didn't turn off the kerosene heater. I told you I did because I wanted to be on time for the track meet. I'm so sorry," she said, falling into her father's embrace.

Over and over, she apologized for not being honest with them. "I know that saying I'm sorry doesn't fix the barn or the things I did and said. But in time I hope to prove to you that I have learned my lesson. From now on, I will always tell the truth, the whole truth, and nothing but the truth. And I will always do my own work in school."

Dad picked up Cassie and carried her into the house. Mother and J.J. followed, as the firefighters made sure that the fire was completely out. They sat at the kitchen table.

"We have a confession to make too," said Dad. Cassie waited for him to tell her what it was. "Meg, do you want to start?"

Mom's eyes filled with tears. "We suspected you were not being truthful with us, Cassie. When we talked to Coach Blevins at the concessions stand Saturday night, we knew for sure that you were not being truthful."

Cassie didn't know what to say. She wished she could just erase this whole chapter from her life. And then Dad said something else. "And about that

California funeral story...we knew that was a little too far-fetched!"

In that moment, Cassie didn't know whether to laugh or cry. But her parents and J.J. began to laugh, so she joined them. After a while, they were laughing and crying.

"We've been praying for you, Cassie," said Mom. "We knew that God would give you the strength to come forward and tell the truth on your own. We know how sorry you must feel, and that you have learned your lesson."

Cassie couldn't believe the love her parents were showing her. They knew she had been lying, and they had been praying for her! It was hard to understand how much love that took or how much pain she had caused them.

"I'm sorry," said Cassie. "I'm sorry it took our old barn burning to realize how lies can catch up with a person. I'm sorry about your woodworking shop, Daddy, and your Christmas present, Mom."

"What Christmas present, dear?"

Dad winked at Cassie. "Don't you worry, Mom. I'm sure we Christmas elves have plenty of time to replace that present."

Cassie decided right then that she had the best family and the best friend in all the world. She also decided to resign from the track team as a member, but she would ask Coach Blevins to allow her to help the team in any way she could. Maybe she could be a water girl! She was sure Missy Foster deserved to be on the girls' track team. Cassie could try out again next year.

In the next few weeks, Cassie Marie Holbrook cleaned up her act. After school, she helped the track team. Then she helped her father rebuild the destroyed wall of the old barn.

Cassie also worked extra hard to earn a C in pre-algebra. And the best part about that was knowing that she didn't cheat or lie to get it. She worked hard for that C, even if it was only an average grade. But she couldn't have been prouder if it had been an A+!

Address: ▼ http://www.mistyfallsfriends.com

Back   Forward   Stop   Refresh   Home   Search   Mail   Favorites

A WHOLE NEW MISTY FALLS WORLD IS READY FOR YOU TO EXPLORE ON THE WEB!

What do Cassie and the gang do in their spare time?

What games do they like to play?

What's going on at Misty Falls Middle School?

What does Misty Falls look like?

**Visit
<u>www.mistyfallsfriends.com</u>
to find out!**

ADVENTURES IN MISTY FALLS

Don't Miss Any of the Adventures of Cassie and the Misty Falls Gang.

Read All the Books!

Cassie, You're a Winner!
1-56309-735-4
N007116
$4.99 retail price
$1.99 through 12/31/00

Robyn Flies Home
1-56309-764-8
N007106
$4.99

Best Friends Forever?
1-56309-734-6
N007117
$4.99

Robyn to the Rescue
1-56309-451-7
N007109
$4.99

J.J., Navajo Princess
1-56309-763-X
N007105
$4.99

Tell the Truth, Cassie
1-56309-452-5
N007110
$4.99

Look for books 7 and 8—available in April 2001!